Abduction Seduction

HER DESIRES ARE
OUT OF THIS WORLD

D.J. RUSSO

ABDUCTION SEDUCTION

Copyright @ 2022 by D.J. Russo

All rights reserved. No part of this book may be used or reproduced in any manner whatsoever without written permission except in the case of brief quotations embodies in critical articles or reviews.

Thank you for buying an authorized edition of this book and for complying with copyright laws by not reproducing, scanning, or distributing any part of it in any form without permission. You are supporting writers and their hard work by doing this.

"I know how alone you feel… alone in all that cold blackness. But I'm there in the dark with you."
Lindsey Brigman
The Abyss

For my husband

Author's Note

Hi there! Thanks for picking up *Abduction Seduction*. I just wanted to give you a quick head's up about the content that's present in the book. This story involves a polyamorous quad (m/m/f/f) and features a lot of graphic, on-page sex. All of the sexual encounters on the page are consensual, but if you aren't up for erotica with aliens who look like aliens, this book may not be for you. Though it's considered erotica, it has an HEA at the end.

If it's helpful to you, I put a full list of content warnings at the back of the book. Be warned, however, it's full of spoilers. Thanks so much for reading, and I hope you'll enjoy the story!

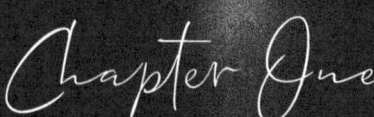

Chapter One

I stare down into the soft blue glow of my phone, unable to comprehend the text I'd just received. My hands tremble until the phone slips from my hand and onto the floor. Fortunately, the hotel room has wall-to-wall carpeting, and it lands with a soft thud. My roommate and best friend, Amber, bursts through the bathroom doorway.

"Taryn? What's the matter? Did something happen?" She asks as she dabs at her damp hair with a towel. I swallow the lump in my throat as I bend over to scoop up my phone and read the text again, this time more slowly. I still can't believe what I'm reading.

"Brandon just broke up with me over a text." My heart slams into my chest as the realization washes over me in measured, violent waves. "He is *actually* breaking up with me over a text!" I shriek before taking another mechanical bite of my stale blueberry scone. It turns to ashes in my mouth. The hotel boasted an amazing free continental breakfast, but all I could find this morning were crumbs, bits of congealed scrambled eggs, and suspicious-looking rubbery bacon. The stale scone was the best of the offerings, so I grabbed it and a cup of lukewarm coffee back up to my room to get ready for the day. I'd just gotten out of the shower and was still wearing a towel when the text came in with a cheery pling-plong noise. My boyfriend of the past five years, breaking up with me to the chime of the most hilariously sunny sound I'd ever heard. Now whenever I recall this moment, I'll think of that stupid sound first.

Amber has been my best friend since kindergarten and has gone to battle for me many times over the years. So, I'm not surprised when she shrieks and nearly drops her coffee all over the bed. She plops the cup down onto the nightstand and sits next to me on the bed. I'm too stunned to do anything other than stare straight ahead at the wall. She narrows her eyes, plucks the phone from my hand, and reads the text out loud. My insides wither as I toss the sad little pastry into the waste bin. I can't finish it. The awful food already ruined my appetite that morning, but this just killed it for good.

"What the hell?" Amber says as she glances back at me, incredulous. "Dear Taryn, I know what I'm about to say is going to come as a shock, and I apologize for that. We've been together for five years, but I have to be honest. I'm just not feeling it anymore. I really hope we can still be friends. Love, Brandon." She twists around on the edge of the bed and gapes at me. "This is ridiculous. Maybe someone else wrote this as a joke?"

I shrug. The breakup isn't actually *that* much of a shock. What's a shock is getting a text message instead of an honest, face-to-face discussion. You know, the kind that adults have? Such an asshole. I naïvely believed I was worth that much to him after half a decade of living together, but I guess not.

"I knew something was off. He was way too chill about you rooming with me this weekend instead of with him," Amber says, her cheeks flushing red. She's angrier about this than I am, which is honestly pretty sad.

Amber finally notices my lack of rage and lofts an eyebrow. "You're not pissed about this? Are you in shock, maybe? Oh, babe. You're in shock."

She wraps her arms around my middle and squeezes me in a satisfyingly tight hug. While being squished by the power of love, I inhale deeply and catch a whiff of her shampoo. Her entire head smells like old lady perfume. It's kind of like a sprig of lavender got into a brawl with a cinnamon stick.

There are no victors, here. Amber has never been a floral scent kind of girl, but we didn't realize until we were twenty miles outside of Philly that we forgot to pack toiletries.

"Amber, I love you, but you smell terrible," I say.

She releases me, shoots me a look of feigned offense, and rolls her eyes. "It's all they had in there! You're deflecting, by the way. Seriously though, are you okay? I'm really worried about you."

I raise a shoulder in a limp half-shrug. "Not really. I mean, yes and no. Yes, I'm in shock because I fucking deserved a better break up than a text." Just saying "break up," and "text," in the same sentence is enough to make me shudder in revulsion. "But no, I'm not that shocked because I kind of saw it coming. He's been short with me for the past month and working late nights at the office. I kind of figured he was cheating on me. I don't have any proof, but…"

She gasps. "Taryn, why didn't you tell me?"

"I dunno. Didn't feel like going into it with Chimera Con right around the corner. We were busy making plans and packing. I thought maybe if we hung out all weekend long, he'd remember why he loved me in the first place. It sounds really stupid when I say it out loud."

"Sweetie, it's not stupid. You were just optimistic. Brandon is trash for doing this to you. We need to confront his ass and demand an explanation."

I can't help but smirk a little. To Amber, it's always "we." As in, "we need to demand why you weren't given a promotion," and "we need to find out why he dumped you over text." She always assumes ownership over my problems, even when they have nothing to do with her. God, I love this woman, but I can't have her stressing out over me all weekend long. She's been looking forward to the con all year, too.

I shake my head and grab my phone out of her hand.

"Nah. This is all me. Don't worry about it," I say as I look down at the screen.

Five years. Five long years, and all I get is a shitty text. What a spineless boyfriend he turned out to be. How difficult was it to break up with someone, a person you planned on marrying someday, in person?

"Taryn. You need to go talk to him. Maybe he's losing his mind because of the doctorate, you know? Remember, he was complaining about his advisor a few weeks ago? He can't end things like this. He *needs* you."

I burst into laughter. I can't help it. He *needs* me? He needs me like a fish needs a bicycle. If anything, he needs less of me riding his ass over every single thing. For the past year, I felt less like a girlfriend and more like a parent to an overgrown toddler. Back at our shared apartment in Philadelphia, I cooked all our meals, paid our rent, did all his laundry, and reminded him about important dates. He needed to understand what it was like being his partner. If he did, maybe he'd have realized just how terrible it was to be with him the past year. After all, I have my own career to worry about even if things on my vlog were stagnating and my work colleagues have started taking me for granted.

"Amber, I love you, but no. He just ended things over a text after five years in which I did everything except wipe his ass. He doesn't need me. I was his enabler."

Amber opens her mouth but shuts it when I shoot her a look. "Sorry. You're right. Remember the time when you asked him to pitch in more at the apartment and his answer to that was scooping the litter box once?"

She didn't have to say anything, but I appreciate the effort. Well-meaning as she is, telling her best friend to go fight for her asshole because he "needs her" isn't my flavor of feminism. I don't need that in my life, and I certainly don't need Brandon to be happy. That's settled, then. I won't fight for him. If he couldn't even be assed to do the right thing, then I'd cut him loose.

"What are you going to do, then? We just got here, but it doesn't matter. Do you want to go home? We can. I won't blame you if you do."

I take a deep breath and look down at my towel-clad self. "I'm going to put on my clothes and some makeup. And then I'm going to go to those UFO panels, but without him. You still have your cosplay thing at ten, right?"

Amber smiles. "Yup! At the Holly Holiday Convention Center. You know where it is, right?"

"Yeah. I'll be there, don't worry about that."

Amber gets up from the bed and kisses me on the top of my head.

"Okay. If you need anything, call me. I mean it. I don't care if I'm in the middle of a panel, alright? I'll drop everything and come find you," Amber says. I smile at her and give up a thumbs up. She heads back into the bathroom to finish getting ready. When she's done, she struts around the hotel room in a tight-fitting latex dress that accentuates every single one of her curves. I asked her a million times in the past thirty minutes if she needed help sliding into the damn thing, but she insisted she was fine.

"I will never doubt you ever again," I say as I hold my phone up to take pictures of her by the window. "You look incredible. Seriously, how did you get into that?"

"Baby powder and magic," she says as she bends over, giving me a view of her ample cleavage. Despite my best friend's hotness, I've never wanted her that way. It would be like hooking up with my sister. Amber grabs a pair of bat wings from the chair and slips them on over her shoulders like a backpack.

"Who are you dressed as, again?" I ask.

Amber stares at me, deadpan. "I told you ten times already. Vampire Rosalina from Voluptuous Vampires: Part Six. Are we even friends?"

I toss my empty cup at her, and she squeals as she puts her hands up to block it.

"Very funny. Yes, of course we're friends."

Amber checks the notifications on her phone and twirls a strand of platinum blond hair around her finger. "Alright, I need to get going before I'm late. Unless you want me to cancel? Because I can ditch the parade."

"No! Don't you dare do that! You've waited too long for this. Go have fun. I'll be fine. Seriously," I say as I wave her off. Amber can't miss this. Especially not because of something my ex-boyfriend did. I don't need a babysitter. What I need is more coffee and a distraction.

"Okay," Amber says, finally relenting. She strokes the back of my head like a cat, and I practically purr. I love being touched, even in the nonsexual way. Maybe *especially* in the nonsexual way. Cuddles and hugs are criminally underrated, in my opinion. "But like I said. You need anything, text."

"Thanks. I love you," I say. She grabs her keys and a giant blue tote back with a pop culture reference to some anime she loves. Ever since the ninth grade, Amber has been really into anime and video games. Meanwhile, I went in a completely different direction and became a little obsessed with occultism and cryptids. Despite our differences, she and I have stuck together, for better or worse. We're like an old married couple that way.

Even though we exist in different communities, she comes with me every year to Chimera Con, the annual festival of all things nerdy that takes place over Labor Day weekend. We drove sixteen hours for this, and it cost us both a pretty penny just to be here. We would have flown down, except Amber has a phobia of planes and I'm not willing to put her through that simply for my own comfort. Gas prices are out of control and driving was exhausting, so I'm not about to let something like a shitty breakup ruin the entire trip for us. She gives me one last sympathetic smile and wave, then leaves for her panels.

I get up, drop the towel to the floor and begin to get ready for the day. I walk into the bathroom, put on a brave face in front of the mirror, and grab my concealer wand from my makeup kit.

"Alright, Taryn. Let's do this," I mutter as I smear the yellowish liquid beneath my eye.

I freeze, stare at myself, then immediately burst into tears.

Fuuuuuck.

I cry for what feels like hours until I finally succumb to my heartbreak and flop onto the bed to bury my face in the pillow.

Okay.

So, maybe I *was* in shock after all.

Now everything is hitting me all at once.

While I have no plans to skip the con entirely (knowing how much this weekend cost me eliminates the temptation), I skip the first two panels of the morning to sob and watch reruns of Paranormal Investigators: New York.

Abduction Seduction

I knew it was a good idea to share a hotel room with my best friend instead of my boyfriend. When I was making the reservations, I asked Brandon how he'd feel about not sharing a room this year. Amber had been under a lot of stress in the past six months. She'd been laid off from her high-paying job, kicked out of her apartment, and the woman she was seeing turned out to have a secret family only three blocks away from her parents' house. To add insult to injury, her usual con roommates bailed at the last minute because of finances.

When I told him I wanted to be there for Amber, Brandon readily agreed and said he'd be staying with a few of his friends from university. While I didn't love the idea of him hanging out with his old college buddies, I figured it would be good for us to spend some time apart.

I lean over the sink in the bathroom as I try to swipe my eyeliner into a perfect wing, but end up squiggling the liner all over my cheekbone and have to re-do it three times. I tell myself it's just nerves, but my mind can't stop playing back every single thing Brandon said to me in the past week. I'm looking for clues, any red flags he may have dropped that I missed.

It's pointless. After having a good cry, I decide I'm going to look hot today no matter what. I'm finally happy with my makeup and throw on my favorite black dress, the one with the corset top and billowy skirt that makes me feel like a goth princess on a leisurely stroll through the cemetery. Plus, it has pockets! I made sure to sew them in myself because more dresses need pockets.

The hallway of the hotel is busy, which isn't a surprise. Most hours of the day during the con weekend are frantic and buzzing with energy. In fact, I doubt most of the people who rush past me laughing and screaming have even slept yet. Today marks the first official day of the con, but most people have been here for two nights already. No one ever wants to miss the mixers and themed raves that go on until six in the morning. Despite waking up to one hell of a nasty surprise, I feel pretty good. At least I'm at Chimera Con, my happy place. Snagging a room at one of the big-four hotels isn't easy, and I had to sweet-talk my way into getting one from a stranger on the internet. Being on site has been a dream of mine since I started going to

Con ten years ago, when I was a fresh-faced twenty-year-old straight out of university. It's worth every penny for the sheer spectacle I'm accosted with as soon as I hit the lobby.

"Hi, good morning!" Someone dressed as a giant, orange monster with bushy blue eyebrows chirps at me. I lift my hand to wave back at them as they skip past me, clutching a bottle of vodka in their fuzzy hand. Oh, geez. People here go *hard*.

"Morning," I say back and pull out my phone. I dig through the official Chimera Con app to figure out where I'm going for my first panel. Doctor Ethan Godwick, famed paranormalist and UFO specialist, is speaking at eleven, so I have a little time to kill before then. I wander down to the lobby to soak in the atmosphere, which is really just droves of people in cosplay doing their thing. Then I grab an iced coffee before heading down to Art Avenue, which is chock full of people shopping for new prints to take home. I rarely ever buy anything here, as all the art is way outside my budget, but it's still fun to look around. A few women walk past in super hero costumes and smile at me.

"I love your dress," one of them says as they pass by. I thank her, and turn my attention to a cubicle adorned with several paintings of various science-fiction scenes. Now *this* is my kind of art. There are spaceships soaring through the stars shooting at enemy ships, brightly colored planets orbiting alien suns, and dizzyingly dreamy watercolors of far-off galaxies. My heart flutters when I take in the paintings, then swoon at the price tag. Yeah, no. My wallet cries at the thought of paying that much, but I pluck the artist's card from the little table in front of the cubicle for later. Maybe I'll save up my next few paychecks so I can hang the painting of the galaxy in my apartment.

Ever since I was a child and could read, I've been obsessed with outer space and everything to do with it. Yes, I love the real stuff, the factual scientific reports, the data, the charts. But I've always been drawn to the what-ifs of the universe. Life in other galaxies? Unexplored star systems with awesome alien species? Yes, please. Give it all to me. It was only natural that my interests turned towards the paranormal and the occult at some point, as well. I started lurking on internet forums in the late 90s as a teenager and my fascination morphed into making an entire career out of exploring the stranger parts of life as a cryptozoologist. Yes, that is a real job. Brandon always used to tease me about how I got my computer science degree, only to go into "Bullshit 101." So, as a joke, I started up a vlog several years ago called Pseudoscience 101. As it turns out, people loved my videos just as much as I loved making them and was able to pay the rent every month while still having some money left over for savings. I still kept my day job as a data analyst, but that's not where my heart is. My heart is with the creatures that go thump in the night, and to a lesser degree, ghosts and demons.

As I continue to loiter in front of the paintings, a man, maybe in his early thirties, approaches the cubicle. He's handsome, with a chiseled face I've only seen on television and sandy blond hair that falls into his hazel eyes. He shoves his hands into his jeans pockets as he inches closer into my space. I move out of his way so he can look at the paintings, because he looks like he's actually a serious buyer and I wouldn't dream of coming between an artist and a paycheck. I start to walk away when the man clears his throat and looks my way.

"It's spectacular, isn't it?" The man says. I look over my shoulder back at him, unsure if he's talking to me or someone else. There's no one else around us, and I point to my face like a dork. He smiles widely, giving me a good peek at his twin set of adorable dimples, and nods.

"Um, yeah. It is. The artist is really talented," I say quickly, and that's when I notice the stubble on his jawline. I'm a sucker for stubble, and my throat hitches. Oh damn, he's hot.

"It always amazes me what people come up with. The passion behind all this art is nothing short of miraculous," he adds as he leans forward to take in the painting of the galaxy I was just admiring. "Take this painting for example. The usage of color is extraordinary."

At first, I worry he's about to go on a pretentious diatribe about what the artist's intent was, and I didn't come here for an art lecture. But then he looks up at me with his dazzling hazel eyes and the corner of his mouth turns up in a slight curve.

"What do you think?" he asks.

I swallow. I wasn't expecting him to actually ask me any questions, so I'm caught off guard. I take a tentative step forward and fiddle with my hands because I'm suddenly painfully aware of my limbs. What should I be doing with them? I pick at my fingernails as I try to think of something to say.

"I think the painting is moving. At least, I was," I blurt out, nerves punctuating every syllable. "Moved, that is. It's as though the artist dreamed the painting first, then when they woke decided to commit it to canvas."

He smiles as he mulls over my answer, and my heart hammers in my chest.

"I like that. A painting dreamed of first. Sounds very… romantic," he says, then offers me his hand. I take it, and we shake I mentally note how warm his skin is. When he releases my hand, I fidget and look back at the painting, unable to meet his gaze.

"I'm Aiden."

"Taryn."

"Taryn," he says thoughtfully, trying out my name for himself. "What an unusual name. What is its origin?"

I blink. Honestly, I have no idea, and no one's ever asked me that before, so I pull out my phone and hit the search bar for information. He leans forward with raised eyebrows, and it probably seems like I'm ignoring him. Within seconds, I have an answer.

"English or Welsh, I think? It says it means 'thunder' or 'from up on a rocky hill.'"

"Are you?" he asks.

I stare up at him and tilt my head, a habit of mine since I was a toddler. My mom used to laugh and tell me I looked like a confused puppy when I did it.

"Excuse me?"

His grin widens. "From up on a rocky hill."

The hunter green t-shirt he's wearing clings to his body like saran wrap, exposing every one of his muscles in ways I can't even comprehend. Why is a guy like this talking to a woman like me? I mean, I know I'm pretty, but I still can't understand his keen interest.

"Not really. I mean, Bucks County is full of hills, but I can't say I'm from a rocky one. Are you familiar with Philly at all?" I ask, grasping for a conversational topic.

He furrows his brow and folds his arms across his brawny chest. "Can't say I am. Say, would you like to join me later for lunch? I'm not sure what you have going on today, but I was thinking we could maybe meet up around eleven-thirty? Gives us time to scope out a few places before they fill up during the meal rush."

I die a little inside. As much as I want to go to lunch with Aiden, I made a promise to myself first that I wouldn't miss a single panel this year. I've already missed two on account of Brandon. I don't break promises, especially to myself, so I'm already starting the con off on the wrong foot. I smile sadly and shake my head.

"I'm sorry, but I have this panel at eleven," I explain. He nods, but I can tell from his expression he's disappointed. Yeah, so am I. He has no idea how bummed out I truly am. A hot guy like him doesn't come around often, and I'm up for a quick rebound hookup.

"Which panel is it?"

Immediately, I'm on the defensive. Whenever I bring up Ethan Godwick, I'm met with blank stares. It's worse when I start to actually explain what he's all about. Alien encounters, UFOs, cryptid sightings. It usually leads into derisive remarks, condescending chortles, and then before I know it, I'm defending my whole damned career to a stranger I'll never see again. He notices I'm floundering, and the dimples are back in full force as he smiles.

"Sorry. If it's none of my business, just let me know and I'll drop it," he says.

I don't want him to think I'm being rude, so I shout, "No! It's not that!" a little too quickly. "It's just that most people think it's weird when they find out I'm into the paranormal track here at the con."

Aiden leans back and shoves his hands into his pockets. He looks...

bemused? Bewildered? I don't know. I can't figure him out. Luckily, he breaks the silence before I have to scrounge up some sort of excuse to swap topics.

"May I go with you?" he asks.

I blink as my jaw opens and closes. "Um…"

"Too forward? Forget about it. I didn't have anything else to do for a little while. My friends are doing their own thing for now, so I figured—"

"Sure. Come with me. The more, the merrier."

I chuckle and pray he doesn't notice just how nervous I am right now. An incredibly attractive man approaches me, barely says three words, and invites himself along to a panel? With *me*? I'm giddy.

"Great." He holds up his wrist and checks his watch. I'm impressed he even has a watch. Most folks just use their phones to check the time. "We have ten minutes to get there. I trust it isn't too far away?"

"It's not," I say, and lead him away past tables brimming with fairy houses and miniature trees. "But we should hurry if we're going to get halfway decent seats."

Chapter Two

Aiden and I squeeze past a crowd of people in the doorway, only to see two available seats in the entire conference hall. Rows upon rows of people wait as Chimera Con staff test the mics at the podium in front of the room. It won't be long now before Ethan Godwick makes his appearance. Staffers close the doors behind us as we enter. We made it just in time.

"Lucky us! I assumed we'd be standing in the back," I say with a small chuckle. I push some of my dark hair behind my ear as I sit down. Aiden looks around the room with wide eyes. His mouth is open, like he's about to speak, but no. He's just *that* impressed with how many people turned out to hear Ethan speak. I'm not. I should have lined up at least an hour ago, but because I was talking with Aiden, I took my chances of being late.

He looks back at me and gives me one of those boyish grins again. When he first spoke to me, I thought he was going to end up being an asshole, or maybe just boring. Aiden is neither of those things. On our way over to the hall, he couldn't stop talking about a cosplay contest he was 'privileged' enough to witness. It was endearing to listen to him go on and on about his favorite costumes, and I nodded along as he barely stopped to take a breath.

"Wow, this is amazing, Taryn. I'm impressed. This man must have made quite the mark on humanity."

The way Aiden speaks is strange, but I'm willing to overlook it because so far, he hasn't raised any red flags, a real rarity these days. Besides, I think it's kind of cute. Maybe he's just really into historical movies and fiction or something. I smile back at him as he continues to marvel at the room, and then everyone in the crowd goes silent. Another staffer walks up to the microphone podium and checks to make sure it's working one last time. An enormous boom erupts from the microphone, and everyone claps their hands over their ears, except for Aiden, who is still just sitting there with the goofiest smile plastered on his face. Yeah, I'd say the audio works, thanks.

"Sorry, sorry," the man says into the mic, then quickly hurries off to find a seat. Within moments, the familiar frame of Ethan Godwick walks to the center of the room. His hair is a riot of salt and pepper and impeccably groomed, and the crinkles in the corners of his eyes are deep. They make his eyes appear friendly, and he's dressed in a gray suit paired with an amusing tie with a couple of astronauts eating pizza on it. Aiden watches Ethan with rapt interest, but he isn't smiling anymore.

"Hello Chimera Con! Lots of your smiling faces out there this morning! Did any of you get any sleep?" Ethan asks. The crowd laughs.

"Ethan, we love you!" a woman behind us screams. Aiden raises an eyebrow at me, and I shrug. I don't get the fanaticism either, but some people are just really passionate. I mean, I'm passionate, just not 'scream your love for a stranger' kind of passionate. He goes back to listening to Ethan as he introduces himself, his thirty-year career, and all of his accomplishments. Aiden folds his arms in front of his chest and narrows his eyes. He's really enthralled by the talk, which is strange to me considering he didn't seem to know who Ethan even was before I told him. But I like the way he gives his full attention to the person speaking. Brandon used to talk over me a lot until I'd almost be in tears, so it's refreshing to encounter a guy who just… listens. The crowd is quiet, save for the occasional overly excited person screaming their affection for Ethan.

After an hour, the talk is finally over and Ethan exits the room. A few people grumble beside us about how fast he left the room, and how they wished he'd at least stay for pictures, but I get it. If he did that, he'd probably be here all day. Aiden is tense beside me, and I see he's digging his fingernails into his thighs.

"Aiden? Are you alright?" I ask. He shifts in his seat and then looks at me with a muted expression.

"Oh, yeah. I'm fine. How are you?" he asks. I raise an eyebrow. Okay, strange. He definitely did not look 'fine' just a second ago.

"I'm good. So, what did you think of the talk? Really informative, right?" I ask as I twirl a single strand of hair around my finger. We don't bother getting up from our seats yet, as there's a queue just to leave the room. He shrugs limply and purses his lips.

"It was, uh… interesting. Thank you for bringing me. I've learned a lot," he says.

"Yeah?" I tilt my head. Yeah, no. I don't believe him. He hated the panel. It's obvious from the look on his face. I was afraid of this happening. I swallow the lump in my throat as I think of a way to salvage the moment when my stomach gurgles.

"I guess we could grab lunch now if you still want to," I say. That finally gets a smile out of him, and he brushes a strand of hair away from my eyes. His gesture is so quick I don't even have time to process it. He takes a deep breath and looks around the room again.

"I would enjoy that, but I'm afraid I need to meet up with my friends. I told them I would find them as soon as I finished up in Art Avenue, but it seems I've taken a bit of a detour on account of a very beautiful woman," he says.

My skin prickles with heat, and for a second I forget how to speak. He's flirting, which is not exactly unfamiliar territory for me, but in the past, it was always easy to skirt around it. I had a boyfriend, so normally I'd have to let someone down easily. Not this time. This time, I have no excuses. Well, I was thinking about a rebound hookup…

"Oh," I start to say, flustered.

"But you should come meet them if you're free. They're really nice, I promise. They're just off doing their own thing. I think Sara wanted to watch a video game tournament of some sort?"

I'm surprised he still wants to hang out with me, but I'm glad he does. He's hot, sure, but he's not *just* hot. He's also sweet and fun to be around. I find myself smiling more while I'm around him because his positive attitude is just so infectious. Plus, I haven't thought about the breakup text since meeting him. I'm afraid that if I go solo now, I'll wind up sitting at the bar throwing myself a pity party. Nah, fuck that. I'm here to have fun, dammit.

"I'd love to meet them," I blurt out.

Aiden nods, and when he stands up, he offers me his hand. I take it, and we leave the conference hall with our fingers laced together. As soon as we walk through the doorway, my heart drops into my stomach. In front of me, standing beside a white pillar next to the drinking fountain, is Brandon. My entire body tenses as I stand in the middle of the doorway, staring at him. Aiden pauses and looks in the direction of my gaze. Brandon is on his phone texting someone and hasn't bothered to look up yet. I could walk away right now and just drop the whole thing, pretend I never even saw him. But I can't. I drop Aiden's hand and trudge up to my ex and stop right in front of him. He still doesn't realize I'm there, like I'm invisible. I clear my throat, and then he looks up from the blue glow of his phone.

He frowns and shoves the phone into the back pocket of his jeans. He winces, and suddenly I'm painfully aware that I'm probably about to cause a scene, because the anger roiling within me doesn't want to be contained. It wants to bubble and froth over regardless of how many people are standing in the hallway. Fucking Brandon and his stupid, beautiful, dark brown beard and sweet brown eyes. No matter how many times we'd get into a fight, I'd always end up prematurely forgiving him because his sad puppy-dog eyes would make me feel bad. I'm determined not to let him win this time.

"A text, Brandon?" I say, the irritation rife in my voice.

Brandon sighs and looks down the hallway, like he's looking for someone to come save him.

"I didn't want to do it in person for this exact reason, Taryn," he says.

I glare at him. "For what reason, exactly?"

"Oh, you know what reason, come on," he huffs and folds his arms in front of his chest as he leans back against the pillar.

"No, no. I don't know. Please enlighten me," I say, mimicking his stance and crossing my own arms.

He rolls his eyes. "I knew you'd make a scene," he murmurs.

"A scene?" I blink. My eyes start to sting. Dammit, why was I letting him get to me like this? "This is hardly a scene, Brandon. I literally said one thing to you. One. I haven't even raised my voice."

He shifts uneasily against the pillar and looks back at Aiden, who is still standing by the doorway. "Who's your friend?" he asks.

I notice the deflection and decide not to take the bait. "Why did you break up with me via text? What's the real reason? We were together for five years. Five. That's a long time, Brandon. Since grad school. I'd like to think I deserved better than a crappy text sent before coffee."

He scoffs. "Would having coffee have made it any better? Or how about if I broke up with you in person, would it have made it any better?"

I tense. "Well, no, but—"

"Then what does it matter if I broke up with you over text or not? The result is the same, right?"

I frown, then nibble on my bottom lip. "That's not fair, and you know it. You could at least give me some sort of closure."

He raises his arms and lets them fall back to his sides with a clap. "Closure. What is there to say? That we weren't right for each other? That we barely saw one another? That you haven't been happy in a while, so I probably just did you a solid by dumping you? We're both still young. You'll find someone else. Someone better."

I open my mouth to speak, but Brandon keeps going. "Look, I'm going back up to Philly a day earlier than planned. The boys are going to help me pack up my shit so I can move in with Todd. You won't even have to deal with me when you get home. So just let me go, please. Go enjoy the con, or whatever."

With that, Brandon strides off towards a group of his friends at the end of the hallway. I don't recognize them, and I don't go after him. What else is there to say? Evidently, five years just dribbled down the drain, and he didn't even seem to care. I bite back the sting of tears that threaten to spill, and Aiden steps beside me. He offers his hand to me again, along with a sympathetic smile.

"I'm sorry you had to see that," I say as I wipe my eyes with the back of my free hand.

"I'm not. But I am sorry that happened to you. You must be in a lot of pain," he says quietly.

I look up at Aiden as my face twists in confusion. "Er… yeah. I mean, I guess? I cried a bunch this morning but I'm feeling better now. I don't know… Brandon was always sort of like this. Domineering in an argument. He always did like to make it seem like it was all my fault, but I know better. At least, I think I do."

Aiden nods. "He was right about one thing, however."

I frown. Oh, shit. Here come those red flags. "How so?"

"You will find someone much better than he is. I'm quite certain of it," he says with a wink. Dammit, why does Aiden have to be like this? I was only planning on trying to hook up with him, but now I'm not so sure. Now I'm actually considering a friendship with this guy, because he seems pretty alright. I suppose I could hook up with him and still keep him as a friend, though, right?

"And he was right about another thing. He did you a favor by ending the relationship at the start of the con."

I laugh and flip my hair back over my shoulders. "Hell yeah he did. Come on, let's go meet your friends."

Chapter Three

We find Aiden's friends on the top floor of the hotel in the twenty-four-hour arcade playing a rousing game of Space Invaders. A tall man with a similar build to Aiden's hunches over the arcade cabinet, mashing the buttons at random. A woman leans against the cabinet with a bored-looking frown on her glossed pink lips. Her hair is curly, cotton candy pink, and falls past her shoulders. She's also wearing the cutest mini dress I've seen during the con, which is basically the antithesis of mine. It clings to every curve of her frame and plunges over her breasts to show off just the right amount of cleavage. I could never wear something like that, but I love seeing the look on other women.

"Wes, Sara," Aiden says as he approaches them from behind.

"Shit," Wes mutters under his breath as he loses the round of Space Invaders. The GAME OVER text pops up on the screen. He spins around and locks eyes with me. He doesn't even look at Aiden, who is standing right there. Wes has bright blond hair that falls in his blue eyes, and he's wearing a black v-neck t-shirt and dark washed jeans. He looks ready to hit the club, not the arcade corner, but appearances can be deceiving. Especially at Con. Sara leans against the arcade cabinet and grins mischievously, clearly no longer bored.

"Who is this, Aiden?" she asks in a sing-songy voice. Her lavender eyes look me up and down as heat rushes to my cheeks. Oh god, am I blushing? I'm definitely blushing, and I hope she doesn't notice. And she has lavender irises! They must be those cool color contacts I'm too afraid to use because I hate poking my eyeballs.

"This is Taryn," Aiden says. He's still holding my hand, and his friends have definitely taken notice. Both of them look down at our clasped hands and lift their eyebrows at the same time. It's an odd feeling, having a virtual stranger introduce you to a set of other strangers. I'm not his girlfriend. I'm barely even his friend, and yet being introduced to them feels good, like this is the beginning of something really special. At least, I hope it is. Maybe I lost one relationship this weekend, but I could potentially come out of it with three new friends. I'm still pissed and a little heartbroken by the whole Brandon situation, and I haven't allowed myself to fully process it yet, but the distraction is nice.

I raise my hand in a little wave and smile at the two of them. "Hi, it's nice to meet you," I say.

Wes and Sara both smile and say their hello's before turning back to Aiden to grill him. "Where'd you two meet?" Wes asks.

"We leave you alone for a couple of hours and you already made a new friend!" Sara exclaims.

Aiden shakes his head slowly, but he's grinning so he can't be too upset with their prodding. Their familiar teasing warms my heart and reminds me of Amber. She and I get on each other's cases like this all the time.

"Yes, I know. We met in Artist Avenue. She was taking a particular interest in some lovely galaxy paintings. I found them compelling. Then we went to a talk by an Ethan…" he looks to me for help.

"Godwick," I say. Wes and Sara share a dubious look and I raise an eyebrow. "Is that bad, or something?"

Sara tosses her cotton candy hair behind her shoulder and puts one perfectly manicured hand on her hip. Her rosy lips peel back into a thin line. "He doesn't have the best reputation with…" she trails off, like she isn't sure if she wants to finish her sentence. I really want to hear what she has to say, though, and can't help but push my luck.

"With?" I finish for her.

"With our community, I guess you could say," she says.

"Wait, what do you mean?" I ask. I've never heard anything aside from glowing praise for Ethan. Those who've met him say he's a really great guy, someone who has been known to sit down for coffee breaks with his employees just to hang out. Okay, yes, he's a multi-millionaire with several properties across the United States and Europe, which isn't the greatest. But he's not like that. He's a good person, and he doesn't even like it when you call him 'Doctor Godwick' because it sounds too stuffy.

Sara shifts her weight from side to side as she glances past me, like she's too uncomfortable to continue the conversation, but Wes isn't.

"The dude is a fraud," he says bluntly. "Doesn't even understand how wormholes work."

I blink and look up at Aiden, who is gnawing on his bottom lip with so much anxious energy I can't help but feel it billowing off him in thick, dark clouds.

"Oh. Well, I suppose he's not for everybody." I laugh nervously and scratch the back of my head. This is off to a terrific start. Aiden's friends hate my hero, which means they'll probably wind up hating me, too. And what does he mean, he doesn't know how wormholes work? He's written several papers on the subject. I wonder what Wes knows that Ethan doesn't. Probably not much. I want to turn around and head back to my hotel room, but Aiden surprises me when he grazes the small of my back.

"I found his talk very interesting," Aiden says, to the surprise of his friends. They look at him like he just declared his love for polka dubstep, if such a thing even exists. "It would be beneficial for us to learn all that we can while we're in the city. That means partaking in panels that might not be our usual interests."

He and Wes stare at one another for a long moment. Sara clears her throat and looks at me again and smiles. I smile back, unsure of what to say. This is awkward. I don't want to come between Aiden and his friends, especially when I literally just met the guy, and I definitely don't love the judgmental vibes I'm feeling right now.

"Do you have any other interests? Cosplay? Games?" she asks sweetly.

I shrug. "Well, I really like the occult, paranormal, and cryptids. UFOs. Alien abduction stuff. That sort of thing. I have a lot of those panels I want to sit in on later today. I don't really game, though. I had a video game console when I was a kid, but that was pretty much it. I suck at them."

"So does Wes, but for some reason he won't let us move on to something else." Sara gives Wes a pointed look, and he glares back at her.

"Perseverance is typically regarded as a desirable trait," he snaps.

"Yes, in times of strife and hardship. In this case, it's just annoying," she quips back. I can't help but giggle at the two of them. I love their chemistry. I can tell they're good friends. Or maybe they're dating? Who knows, it's not my business either way, but I can tell a solid friendship when I see one.

I glance back up at Aiden, who isn't chewing his lip anymore, thank goodness. I was starting to worry he was going to chew his face off at the rate he was going. I squeeze his hand and he smiles as strands of hair fall in his eyes. He's too tall for me to brush them away, but I want to. I really, really want to.

"Sorry about them, they can be rather… childish at times," he says as he shoots Wes and Sara a stern look. I laugh and raise my shoulder in a half-shrug.

"Oh, please! Don't stop on my account. It's fine. Amber and I are the same way," I say.

Wes leans back against the arcade cabinet like a relaxed panther in a tree and asks, "Who is Amber?"

"My best friend. She's here, too, but she's into entirely different stuff, so she's at her panels for the day while I'm just sort of floating around until the next panel."

Wes grins at Aiden. "Ah, now I see why you latched onto her. She was like a stray kitten wandering the Art Avenue all alone and you decided to bring her home with us."

I blink. I have no idea what Wes is going on about, but I'm definitely no stray kitten.

"You make it sound like I'm lost. I'm not lost, I'm just... enjoying the con by myself," I add quickly. Aiden runs his thumbs along my palm and the hairs on the back of my neck stand at attention. I feel safe when I'm around him, but I know that letting my guard down around a guy I just met is also not the wisest choice. My mother taught me better than that. Never leave drinks unattended, stay in public areas when meeting someone new, don't assume everyone who is nice to you is a good person. Check, check, check.

Wes smiles apologetically at me and shrugs. "I'm sorry. I didn't mean anything bad by it. I just meant that our Aiden here has a big heart."

This isn't sounding much better. "Well, I'm not a charity case, either."

"Stop talking, Wes, before I have to go find you a shovel," Aiden warns. His voice is thick and rumbly, like a low growl. Suddenly I'm picturing what he sounds like in bed, with the lights dimmed and a few scented candles lit on the dresser. His rumbling voice telling me all the ways he wants to ruin me six ways from Sunday, all the while his hand is between my thighs rubbing my clit...

"What do you think, Taryn?" Aiden asks, interrupting my fantasy. My cheeks are flushed and the tingling between my legs is now full-on wetness. Oh, god. I was just fantasizing about getting fucked by this stranger in front of his friends. Time and place, Taryn, for real.

"I'm sorry, what?" I ask as I look around the group. They're all staring at me, and I'm embarrassed to think they'd been having a full-blown conversation while I was off having wet daydreams by myself. *Ugh.* Wes comes to my rescue by pointing to the row of rhythm games that line the back wall. There's a bunch of people playing, their bodies bouncing up and down in tandem to the beats. I haven't seen a rhythm game since the early 2000s, so it's pretty exciting that they have them here. I've only ever played on a dance mat, so seeing the whole metal setup is impressive. There are so many flashing lights! I smile wide and look back at Wes and Sara and nod.

"Oh, are we playing? I love Dancer's Rhythm Paradise. I used to play it when I was younger," I say as Aiden tugs me towards the machines. We get in queue and wait our turn until we're finally up. All four of us ascend the metal machines, pick our songs, and start pounding our feet on the arrows. I'm rusty, so I miss a lot of the arrows on the screen, but it doesn't matter because I'm having a blast. Wes nearly topples over onto the ground after missing a combo, and I laugh.

"Wes, you can hold onto the back bar if it's too much for you," I say. He rolls his eyes at me, but he places his hands on the back banister anyway. Aiden is slow on his machine, but he's doing his best and doesn't miss as many of the combos as I would have expected. Meanwhile, Sara is dazzling the crowd that's gathered behind us. Her pink hair sways as she moves her hips back and forth to the song. She's a real dancer, I can tell, and she's absolutely crushing her score. Once the song has ended, people behind her clap and cheer. I look over at her and join the applause.

"Damn, Sara! This isn't your first time with DRP, is it?"

Sara tosses her hair back in a beautiful pink cascade and laughs. It sounds so feminine and melodic, my gut wrenches. I start to imagine what kissing her would feel like. Her lips look so soft, and they probably taste sweet thanks to that sheer pink lip gloss she's wearing. As she laughs, her breasts heave, making her cleavage much more prominent. It's hard not to notice them, but I also don't want to be creepy, and I force myself to avert my gaze. Her breasts are perky handfuls, a stark contrast to my F cups. I love my breasts, always have, but there's something about a woman with smaller breasts that really does it for me. I bet finding cute bras that fit is really easy for her, too. I'm simultaneously aroused and envious, one of the rare annoyances of being bisexual.

"No, actually. First time," she says as she steps off the machine to let someone else have a turn.

"No way! You looked like a total pro up there," I say as I move to the side. Aiden and Wes jump off the platforms of the machines and join Sara and me as we head towards the board games tables.

"Thanks. I really love to dance. It's one of my favorite things to do when I'm—"

Wes shoots her a look that tells her to shut up. I have no idea why, though, and blink.

"When you're what?" I ask, too curious to let it go. She shrugs.

"Oh, nothing! But yeah, I love dancing!"

Aiden scoops up my hand and pulls me towards him. I'm stunned by the intimacy of the action, and I let out a nervous giggle. He leans over to whisper in my ear, and goosebumps prickle on my arms.

"If you want to go dancing later—for real, this time—I can take you," he whispers. A chill runs down the length of my spine at the proximity of his body and the mere suggestion of being held by him on the dance floor. I nod enthusiastically.

"I would love that!"

The four of us quit the room and head downstairs to find something to eat. When we can't find even a single place that serves coffee, we brave the crowds on the hot, muggy streets of the city. I cringe when we pass through the doorway and step out onto the pavement. There are people everywhere. Con-goers shuffle on the sidewalk shoulder to shoulder, which would be uncomfortable no matter what the circumstances were, but today it's over 95 degrees and the sunlight is direct. My companions all wear the same look of despair as sweat beads on our foreheads instantaneously.

"We have to cross the street at the corner, then head over there for the food court," I say as I point to the adjacent hotel. So close, and yet so far. It feels like walking through pea soup right now. Despite the heat, Aiden still insists on holding my hand. I'm not complaining, but I do wish we could get through the crowds faster. On a normal weekday, it would only take us thirty seconds to make it across the street and into the hotel, but today it takes over twenty minutes. Once we're finally in the lobby of the other hotel, we all heave a collective sigh of relief when the air conditioning slams us in the face upon entering.

"I thought I was going to die out there," Sara says, panting.

"I know. It's always hotter than balls in the south during this time of year. It's lovely in November, though," I say as I push the matted clump of wet hair away from my forehead. Wes grimaces as sweat trickles down his neck in long rivulets. Despite being sweaty messes, my friends are all still staggeringly attractive. I catch a glimpse of myself in a mirror as we make our way towards the escalators, and I wish I could say the same for myself. I look awful and could really use a freshening up, but that will have to wait. My mascara is forming unpleasant rings underneath my eyes and my concealer is getting flaky. But there's no way I'm leaving Aiden and his crew now, not when we just started getting to know one another. All the lines to the bathrooms are at least a thirty-minute wait. No, thanks. I'll deal with raccoon eyes.

Once we're in the food court, Wes runs up to a Happy! Happy! Burger and grabs a stack of napkins and hands them to me, as though he read my mind moments before.

"Thought you might want these after being outdoors," he says as he hands me the stack. I take them and thank him.

"That's really thoughtful, Wes. Thanks."

A few women in tight pleather dresses stop dead in their tracks to watch Wes as he runs his fingers through his hair. They whisper something to one other, and Wes plants a hand on his waist as he grins at the women.

"Like what you see?" he asks. The girls trot off in a cacophony of giggles. I hadn't noticed it in the arcade, but Wes is really handsome. All three of them look like they just stepped off a red carpet event in Hollywood. A man dressed as a chimera wiggles and dances around in the center of the food court. He's handing out leaflets for something, so I go up to him and take one. Aiden appears behind me to read over my shoulder.

"Ah, a blood drive?" he asks with mild interest. "Perfect. I would like to visit that later."

"Really?" I raise a brow as I hand him the leaflet. Wes and Sara grab two of their own and read them together.

"Yes. I think it's important to give back to those in need," he says.

I agree, but I've never actually given blood before. Normally, needles freak me out. It's not that I have a phobia of them, I'm just disturbed by anything medical. I even have a little bumblebee tattoo on my foot, so needles are fine. But when I was a kid, I had a pretty traumatic experience while my father was in the ER for a blood clot in his leg and I've never been able to shake the revolting feeling I get whenever I drive past a hospital.

Okay, so maybe I *do* have a tiny phobia. The look on my face must tell him enough, because he hands the leaflet back towards me and grins. "But if you don't want to, we certainly don't have to. I can always hit it up later."

Oh, fuck it. He's right. It's important to give back, and what's the worst thing that can happen? I get dizzy and need to sit and eat some free cookies?

"No, I'm in. Let's do it," I say with a confident smile. Wes and Sara both nod.

"We're in, too," Wes says.

"Great, but let's get something to eat first so I don't pass out. I've never actually done this sort of thing before," I say as I point to a burrito place at the end of the food court. I'm not sure why I readily agreed to having my blood taken. I've been acting purely on gut instinct ever since this morning, which isn't something I normally do. Usually, I end up talking myself out of things, or just going with what Brandon wanted to do. Making impulsive decisions all day has only worked in my favor so far, so what's the harm in keeping up the lucky streak? Besides, it's not like I have anything else going on, what with Amber off doing her own thing and my relationship nose diving into the concrete this morning. But there's also another niggling feeling at the back of my mind telling me to slow down and take stock of the situation. Maybe I'm being a little *too* impulsive, but it feels way too good to stop.

Chapter Four

The blood drive isn't as busy as the rest of the con, which doesn't surprise me. Even with all the hard-working volunteers trying their best to woo potential donors with exclusive Chimera Con swag, it doesn't pull in the numbers like the other booths around us. The four of us get in line behind a few people who are wearing Chimera Con blood donor t-shirts from previous years. Aiden and I stand side by side in line. I give his hand a gentle squeeze and look up at him. He's not looking at me, though. He's looking straight ahead at the staff members weaving in and out of the tightly drawn curtains.

"Are you okay?" I ask him, and he finally drags his gaze down to meet mine. He nods.

"Fine, why?"

I shrug. "You just seem a little nervous, is all."

He chuckles and I watch the gentle bob of his Adam's apple. The way he swallows even seems nervous, and I'm wondering if I made a mistake in coming down here with them. Wes and Sara bicker behind us over what's the best meal to eat after giving blood. Wes is team pizza, while Sara thinks having something lighter like orange juice and fruit is the better option. I really have no stake in this at all, so I keep my mouth shut and eyes forward until it's my turn to step forward and register.

A woman with a sleek bob haircut chirps, "Hello!" to the two of us. She's wearing jeans and a Chimera Con staff t-shirt and holds out a clipboard for me to take. I look down at the paper and sigh when I see how long it is. They want every single one of my specs on this sheet, it seems, but I remind myself it's for a good cause. People need blood, and many hospitals deal with blood shortages all the time. My donation could save someone's life, which means a lot more to me than a few minutes of momentary annoyance. I nod and grab one of the pens from the plastic cup the woman holds up to me and start filling out the paperwork when another woman calls Aiden over. He walks over to her, and out of the corner of my eye, I notice him whisper something in her ear. She immediately escorts him away behind one of the curtains. Okay, weird. What was that all about?

"Miss?" the woman's voice breaks my concentration. I look up to find her staring at me, clearly concerned because I just zoned out for several seconds.

"Oh, sorry. I got distracted. Um, it's asking me for my blood type but I don't actually know it," I say.

She smiles. "That's okay! We can tell you afterward if you'd like. We'll find out for you. First time donating, then?"

I nod.

"Okay, well, don't be nervous. It's a wonderful thing you're doing, and we greatly appreciate it! Here's a pamphlet that has all sorts of stats on it if you're curious…" the woman leans over the plastic folding table and plucks one of the pamphlets, then hands it to me. I take half a second to glance at it before smiling back at her.

"Uh, thanks."

"Step this way, and another staff member will be with you soon!" The woman says as she gestures for me to follow her.

Wes is up next, but I'm ushered away so quickly towards a row of chairs facing the curtains I don't have a chance to see what he does. That moment between Aiden and the woman was strange, and now I'm wondering if he got cold feet or felt ill. Thanks to my anxiety, I dig my fingers into my knees before I realize I'm starting to mess up the fabric of my skirt.

"Taryn?" A man with round, fashionable glasses steps forward from behind the curtains. The same curtains that are currently hiding all the scary bits from the prying eyes of the rest of the con. Who even knows what's going on back there right now? My imagination starts to run unchecked and I'm picturing vampires sucking the blood out of their victims behind each one of these curtains. I shiver before looking up at the man, who is smiling at me patiently. That's ridiculous. I know it is. Vampires aren't real, and these people are just doing their jobs.

"Hi, that's me." I stand up and smooth out the lines on my skirt.

"We're all set up for you now! First time?" he asks as he leads me back behind the curtains.

All I see are rows of flat beds filled with people giving blood. Tubes full of red fluid are secured in the arms of the donors, and most of the people look perfectly comfortable. I know that rationally everyone is fine and healthy, but the scene still makes my stomach twist. I don't see Aiden anywhere, though. Okay, definitely odd. Wasn't he giving blood, too? What's the deal? He did look really nervous in line. I wonder if he was too anxious to go through with it after all. If that was the case, he could have just told me. I understand what it's like being afraid of the unknown. Maybe he was worried I'd freak out and not want to go through with the donation myself, though. That would make sense. At least, that's what I want to believe. I sit down on the edge of the bed while the staff member pricks my finger with a little machine I don't recognize for the hemoglobin check. With my free hand, I rifle through the little welcome pamphlet the woman gave me and start reading. After a few minutes, my blood is given the okay and I get comfy on the bed to start the exciting part. The needle doesn't hurt as much as I thought it would, and the entire experience, while a bit boring, only takes about ten minutes.

"Okay, you're all set," the man says with a friendly smile. "We're going to escort you over to the waiting area. We have lots of juice and snacks, as well as some free swag for you to pick up as our way of saying thank you."

I nod and allow him to escort me over to the waiting area where a handful of people are nibbling on crackers and cake. Okay, no one told me that cake would be here. Suddenly I'm thrilled I donated blood. Then I hone in on Wes and Sara, who are cutting themselves some chocolate cake slices. I didn't see them giving blood, but I bound up to them, anyway.

"Hey, you two," I say with a small wave.

Sara's face lights up when she sees me. "There she is! How was it? No wooziness, huh?"

I shake my head. "No, surprisingly I feel… fine? Am I supposed to feel woozy?"

Wes laughs as he slides the cake onto his paper plate. "Most people feel at least a little off. You're a little gold star donor."

I smile. "I didn't see you two give blood. And where's Aiden?"

Sara's face falls as she takes a forkful of cake. "Oh, he had to go to the restroom for a bit. He didn't want to tell you this because he thought maybe you'd think less of him, but the sight of blood makes him faint."

Ah, that explains everything. I knew something was going on, and it was a perfectly reasonable explanation. I keep searching for red flags that aren't there, but I'm going to cut myself some slack thanks to the eventful morning I had.

"I can understand that," I say as I scrape my fingernails against my palm. "I didn't see you two in there either, and you were behind me. Not into the sight of blood either, huh?"

They look at one another and frown.

"We gave blood earlier today, but they remembered us and let us back here," Sara says a little too hastily, like she's trying to cover her tracks. She's lying, I can tell, but I don't want to press her. Something strange is definitely going on, but I don't want to screw up the whole day by getting too nosy. Whatever it is, I'm sure it's none of my business. I go back to eating my cake in silence while Wes and Sara chat quietly. A hand on my lower back sends me spinning around instinctively, my heart wedged in my throat. I come face to face with Aiden's chest, and he smiles apologetically.

"Sorry, didn't mean to scare you," he murmurs.

Seeing him makes my heart flutter, weirdness be damned. The rest of my body tingles with warmth just from seeing him, like I'm being drawn into this guy's gravitational pull. He takes both of my hands into his and holds them gently.

"Are you okay? Donation go alright?" he asks. He's so close to me I can feel his breath against my neck, which only makes me want to take him back up to my hotel room to get this damned sexual tension done and over with so I can enjoy the rest of the con without my ladyboner getting in the way.

"It did, but I wish you'd told me you were skeeved out by blood. It's completely fine. Lots of people are. I don't think any less of you," I say. His eyebrows lift and he takes a step back to look over at Wes and Sara.

"You told her I was scared of blood?" he asks.

Sara smirks and puts a hand on her hip. "She wanted to know what happened to you. I didn't want her to think you ran off and abandoned her."

"I wouldn't do that," he mumbles. "I wouldn't."

I narrow my eyes as I look between the two of them. The air around us shifts and we all fall into an uncomfortable silence. I only just met Aiden, but he's already making declarations about never abandoning me. It's all just a little too strange for my liking, and my gut instinct is telling me to bail and go outside for some air, but I ignore it. My gut has been trying to clue me in all day that going with the flow might not be in my best interest, and I'm suddenly reminded of all the fights Brandon and I had in the past year. The late nights, him telling me everything was fine, that he was just tired. Lies, lies, lies. We were on a trajectory for destruction and I never considered my co-pilot in the relationship might've been feeding me a bunch of lines. I don't know who I can trust anymore, if anyone. For once, I should be listening to my gut and I've been choosing to ignore it because I've been so determined to have fun.

As though sensing my indecision, Aiden puts his arm around me protectively. He looks down at me with the softest expression I've seen him make so far, and for a moment I swore he was going to kiss me. He doesn't.

"I'm sorry. We haven't exactly been honest with you," he says. My heart drops at the same moment Wes drops his cookie on the floor. Sara works her jaw and moves forward to grab his arm.

"Aiden. Stop," she warns. I look between them to find any evidence they're playfully bantering again, but she's serious. I nibble my bottom lip and step away.

"Okay, I don't know what the three of you are into, but I just had my heart exploded this morning and I'm really not in the mood for any weirdness, sorry," I say, my voice shaking. Other people around us eating their cake and cookies stare at us, and my skin pimples on my arms. I was being serious when I said I wasn't in the mood for any weirdness, and I hate having prying eyes in my business. I turn around and walk away towards the lobby. Aiden calls my name, but I don't turn around. They let me go as I wipe a few tears from my eyes. Well, shit. I guess my Chimera Con weekend really is fated to suck, isn't it?

I find a comfy bench to sit on in the middle of the lobby and decide to soothe my aching heart with people-watching. Someone dressed as the Flying Spaghetti Monster waddles past, which gets a few laughs out of me, but I'm still too much of an emotional mess to fully enjoy the scene. I should just go back to my room, cry, order room service and then take a nap. I know it's what I *should* do, so why can't I do it? My mother always said I was chronically stubborn. Chronically, because I'm a 'never surrender' type, which she said was a good thing, but right now I'm not so sure. I slide my phone out of my skirt's pocket and send a text to Amber. She probably won't see it anytime soon. She's having way too much fun at her back-to-back panels, I'm sure, but she's the only person in the entire con who I know won't let me down.

> **TARYN:** I am having the worst con ever.

Within seconds, I see Amber has not only seen my text, but is typing back.

> **AMBER:** Awww sweetie! Is it because of Brandon? I saw him earlier today. You'll be so proud of me. I didn't punch him!

TARYN: Because of Brandon, among other things.

AMBER: Do you want me to come find you? We can talk about it over drinks.

I pause. There's no doubt in my mind Amber would drop everything in her schedule just to come listen to me vent, but again, I don't want to interfere with her good time. It's not her fault Brandon blind-sided me with a breakup and I decided to hang out with a group of hotties I wasn't ready for.

TARYN: No, that's okay. You have fun. Maybe later tonight we can have those drinks, though?

AMBER: Absolutely, sweetie. Stay strong, you got this! Love you!

I smile at the text and put my phone down in my lap to watch a cosplay parade float past in a conga-line. It looks fun, but I'm not in the mood to join in. Just when I start to resign myself to my pity party, Sara slides down onto the bench. I pull back in surprise, then notice she's wearing an expression fit for battle.

"Damn, you're like a cat. I had no idea you were even nearby," I say.

"Look, I understand that we're a lot, especially Wes. But we didn't mean to scare you off, and we definitely want to spend more time with you. I apologize for the shadiness," she says in a single breath. I stare at her because I have no idea what to say in response to any of that. Her shoulders relax, as does the rest of her face. "I'm sorry, Taryn. We were just getting to know each other. Aiden told me about your mate—partner. Ugh. Sorry." She winces, but continues. "Boyfriend. He told me about your boyfriend. That sounds horrible."

I narrow my eyes. She definitely just said mate. Who the hell are these people?

"Yes. It was awful," I say in a far-off voice even I don't recognize. "Where are you from?"

"What?" She blinks.

"Where are you from?" I ask again. I don't detect any noticeable accent that could pinpoint me to any particular part of the United States, but I could be wrong. She could be from anywhere, really.

Wes claps his hands on her shoulders as he appears behind her. She tenses and slams her eyes shut.

"Wes, please," she says sternly. "I'm trying to have a serious chat with Taryn."

Wes flashes me an eager-to-please puppy dog grin. "I can see that. Just thought I'd come over to help a little. Taryn, we like you. Come back to us please, don't leave us all alone!"

I roll my eyes. His pleading is kind of cute, though, so I can't help but smirk. "You're not all alone. There's three of you, remember?"

Wes laughs and there's a twinkle in his eyes that's oddly charming. His is a face I would definitely sit on, but there's still the strangeness surrounding the trio that I can't shake. They might be sweet and fun to be around, but the deception has me majorly concerned.

"Thanks, but I'm not sure if I can deal with more lying by omission stuff," I say. Wes's charming face crumples, and Sara nods as though she was expecting that response.

"I understand, Taryn. And I am sorry about that. We might not be able to tell you everything about ourselves, but we would love to spend the con with you. You've been a lot of fun," she says in earnest. I can tell that part was sincere, at least.

"Where's Aiden?" I ask as I look around the lobby. He's nowhere in sight, and my chest tightens. I only just met him hours ago, but for some reason I'm a little attached to the guy. Just thinking about spending the rest of the con without him makes my stomach flip-flop in a way I don't appreciate.

Sara and Wes grin at each other before answering. "He's around. Off nursing his wounds with a drink at the bar, I'd imagine. He was pretty sad you left. You know, you're the first woman he's taken an interest with in a long, long time."

Wes laughs. "His standards are way too high. I tell him that all the time, but who knows how his brain even works, because I don't."

They're probably just buttering me up so I'll come back to the fold, and I'm ashamed to admit to myself it's working. I roll my eyes with a smile and offer my hand to Sara. She smiles back and takes it before helping me back onto my feet.

"Okay, let's go have fun," I say, and Sara pulls me towards the crowd of excited cosplayers. We weave through lifelike Gundams, a mob of T-Rexes, and a whole lot of lightsabers before reaching the hotel bar. It's crammed full, and the poor bartender looks like he's about to have an aneurysm trying to keep up with all the orders. The chalkboard menu boasts specialty Con drinks and small plates, and some of them look pretty tempting, not gonna lie.

Frustration creeps in when I can't find him right away, and then I spot him. Aiden is sitting at the bar looking dejected while clutching the most adorable frozen cocktail I have ever seen. It's neon blue with a light-up plastic ice cube, and there's a little plastic UFO sticking out of it. He sips the drink through a curly straw while sighing every few seconds.

"Aiden!" Sara shouts, and Aiden twists around to find us in the crowd. His eyes widen when he sees me, and his frown turns into the goofiest, most charming smile I've ever seen in my life. The urge to kiss his dimples sends my libido into overdrive, and I struggle to keep the butterflies fluttering about in my stomach from escaping.

He hops off his stool and heads in our direction. My heart quickens in my chest as he closes the gap between us.

"You're back," he says as he leans forward.

"I'm back."

"I'm sorry for—" he starts, but I shake my head and point to his drink.

"It's okay. Sara already apologized for all three of you. What I want, though, is one of these," I say as I tap his drink.

He laughs and offers me the straw so I can take a sip. It's delicious, freezing cold, and exactly what I need in my life.

"Sold," I say. He takes my hand in his and escorts me back to the bar, with Wes and Sara not far behind.

After drinks, we sit in the middle of the lobby to people watch. It's still as busy as ever despite going on midnight, with no signs of slowing down. I rest my head against Aiden's shoulder, and he practically glows from the sudden, affectionate gesture. We've been holding hands all day like we're pre-teens, and I love it. It's been ages since I've had this much fun, minus the couple of speed bumps along the way. As I sit with my cocktail, I think about the weekend ending and I'm just... sad. I don't want the weekend to end, and I certainly don't want to go home. I want this weekend to last forever, or at the very least, a few extra weeks. I guess what I really need is a break from life in general.

Wes sits with his legs crossed eating an ice cream cone while Aiden points out costumes he's particularly taken by.

"Taryn. We have to tell you something," Sara says as a group of ninja turtles walk past. We watch the turtles and snicker, but she turns back to me. Her mouth is drawn back into a thin line, and her eyes have a sharper glint to them. Oh, shit. This sounds like it's going to be a serious talk, and I'm really not in the mood for serious talks right now. Not when we just started having fun again.

"What's up?" I ask as I mentally prepare myself to be blindsided by something weird. Again.

Wes licks his ice cream and nudges Sara's side.

"Well, here's the thing. What if we told you that we aren't actually... people?"

I stare at her. Aiden's body stiffens against mine. She's making him uncomfortable again, which makes *me* uncomfortable.

"What do you mean by that? Not people? C'mon. You're obviously people," I say, keeping my voice lighthearted. She shakes her head, sending her curls bouncing on her shoulders.

"I mean, we're not human. Nor are we from around here."

I roll my eyes. "I get it, so you're actually vampires, then? That would explain the weirdness at the blood drive. Did you ask one of the staffers to put aside a bunch of O negative for you?"

Aiden doesn't look at me. Wes finishes licking his ice cream and is about to start chomping on the cone when Sara shoots him a glare. He scowls right back at her and crunches into the sugary wafer.

"No, Taryn. We wanted to talk to you about this earlier, but we didn't have a chance. We really like you, and we want to keep spending time with you. But we're aliens, Taryn. We don't want to keep lying by omission, as you put it so well earlier. So, we're going with brutal honesty this time."

I look up at Aiden. He's staring straight ahead, like he's disassociating. That worries me. I touch his forearm, and he snaps his attention back to my face.

"Hey, you alright? It's a funny joke, if that's what you're going for. You got me, ha ha," I say, but I'm not amused. None of this is funny. I just want to go back to drinking and soaking in the con atmosphere. Fat luck there. Sara's cheeks turn bright pink to match her dress.

"I told you she wouldn't buy it," Wes says quietly. Sara shoots him another look, then sighs.

"But we wouldn't lie to you…" Sara says, and she sounds so disappointed I can't help but lean forward and throw my arms around her neck. The last thing I want is for her to be sad, especially not over something so seemingly trivial.

"Hey. I believe you. If you say you're aliens, then you're aliens. It's good enough for me. I don't care if you are or not. Look at who you're talking to. I believe Big Foot is out there somewhere."

I pull away, and she smiles sadly. When I sit back down beside Aiden, he hands me the rest of his drink.

"Can't finish it," he grumbles. Okay, clearly there's some tension here that needs dispelling, stat. I'm not sure what the whole alien business was about, but it's obvious we need a change of scenery.

"So, what else do you all want to get up to tonight?" I ask, flashing them the biggest smile I can.

"Oh, I have a few ideas," Wes says with a sly grin before pushing himself to stand. "Let's get out of here."

Aiden's mouth is on my breast before my shirt hits the floor. I suck in a gasp as his tongue drags around my nipple in slow, agonizing circles. Sara undresses and tosses her jeans onto the chair in the corner of the room. When we had the 'your place or mine?' talk, we decided fucking in my room when I had a roommate who may or may not randomly pop back in at any moment was a bad idea.

I just didn't expect their room to be a penthouse several blocks away from the con itself. I have no idea how they managed to even get this place, what with every hotel and hostel booked solid for months leading up to the event. This must've taken some serious planning, not to mention overflowing wallets, to make this happen.

But right now? None of that matters.

Aiden runs his fingers through my hair as he draws my other nipple into his mouth. Wes, who is already naked, stands behind me and runs his hands down my bare stomach. I can feel his cock, brutally hard with need, pressing against my butt.

"Is this okay?" Wes asks.

My eyes roll into the back of my head. If I could purr, I would. "Yes," I said in between whimpers. Satisfied, Wes tilts my head back gently and presses his lips against mine. They're softer, so much softer than I assumed they would be. In a blur of motion, Aiden whisks me off to the bed to lay against Sara, who is already lounging on her side. She grins at me, and I'm finally given a glimpse of her perfectly round tits without fabric in the way.

"Didn't expect any of this to happen," I say as I run my hand down her side. Her bright eyes widen as she snatches my hand and brings it up to her breast. I caress her skin in light brushes, too timid to get a handful just yet.

"You didn't? We've been flirting all day. I'd say it was an inevitability," she says. I give her breast a gentle squeeze and look back to where Aiden is standing in front of the television. I didn't get a good look at the room after we entered it, on account of being too busy kissing Sara the whole way up the elevator ride. It's pretty swanky, with beautiful floral duvet covers with actual dust ruffles attached. Dust ruffles. I have never owned a dust ruffle in my life.

There's an ornate marble vase next to the television stand that houses some sort of palm-like plant. The entire room smells like those 'fresh linen' candles I never understood, because my fresh linen never smelled like anything. I could never afford a place like this, not even with my decent salary from both my channel and day job. It's just so… opulent.

"Is everything okay?" Sara asks. Wes sits at the edge of the bed and begins stroking Aiden's cock with a tight grip. "Taryn?"

I force myself to look away from the men and smile at Sara, but I know it isn't convincing.

"Sorry. Stimulus overload, I think."

For the past five years, I've slept with Brandon, and only Brandon. Our sex life was always… well, it was fine. I guess. Sometimes I came, sometimes I didn't. Our favorite position—or rather, his—was missionary, with him hammering between my legs until one of us got off (him, of course, and then he'd finish me off with my vibrator). Threesomes were never a thing I'd considered having. Not even in university, when there was a threesome situation happening every night of the week. Now I was in the middle of a foursome, and I wasn't sure what to do.

"It's okay, let's just take it slow for now," she says as she drags her fingernails across my side. "May I touch you?"

I nod. We all had drinks at the bar, but none of us are drunk. No one is getting into a situation with impaired judgment. We checked in with one another several times before getting into the cab. No, I'm doing this without the haze of alcohol, and I intend to make the most of it. Sara shimmies closer to me on the bed and kisses me. Timidly at first, and then harder once she realizes I'm not going to pull away. She cups my cheeks in her hands and cradles them, letting the heat between us grow and grow until it's a raging inferno. Then she positions herself on top of me, and I wriggle against the sheets as her breasts press against mine.

Oh shit, this is hot. Hotter than anything I've ever experienced before, and she's barely touched me.

Brandon wasn't my first, but it's not like I've had a ton of sexual experience before. Sara is the first woman I've been with, and she seems to sense that without my needing to tell her. She's slow, gentle, and asks questions before putting her hands anywhere new.

"May I touch you… here?" she asks as she brushes her fingers against my nipples.

"Oh god, yes," I practically beg. Her mouth is on my tits and sucking before I have time to react. Aiden's groan from the other side of the room pulls my attention away from Sara for a second, just in time to see him toss his head back in pleasure. My cunt is slick with my own need, and Sara's hand is in between my thighs before I have a chance to beg her for the attention.

Aiden locks eyes with me from across the room. His stare is intense and full of lust, and all the thoughts inside my head dribble out of my ears. My brain short circuits as Sara rubs my clit, but she's careful not to press her fingers inside of me. Her fingernails aren't suited for that type of play, but she's a pro and knows her limitations. Within seconds, her head is between my thighs and sucking on my cunt like she's starving. My first orgasm of the evening crashes over me like a wave, and I throw my head back into the pillow as I shout a string of expletives at the ceiling.

But it's not enough.

Wes's head bobs back and forth as he takes Aiden's length to the hilt. Watching porn is one thing, and mostly enjoyable when I can find something suitable. But there's no contest. Watching Wes suck the life out of Aiden is the most erotic thing I've ever had the pleasure of witnessing. Aiden taps Wes gently on the head, and he releases his cock in a thick trail of saliva and pre-cum.

"What's up? You alright?" Wes asks. Aiden nods and stares directly at me.

"Yeah, I'm good. But I think I want to give our princess a proper warm welcome into the group," he says in a thick, gravely voice I haven't heard before. I raise an eyebrow as he makes his way across the room. He's a little less formal in the bedroom, which I like. He's also a lot more commanding, too. Which I really, really like. He climbs onto the bed and positions himself in front of me on his knees. Sara and Wes go to the other bed to have fun with each other, I assume, but I'm not paying attention to either of them. Aiden and his domineering presence completely steal my attention. There's never been a situation in my life where I wanted to be spanked, not ever. But something about the way Aiden looks at me makes me want to bend over and beg for his forgiveness.

Aiden reaches for the box of condoms on the nightstand and pulls one loose. I watch, panting, as he rips open the packet and slides the condom over the tip of his cock and down the rest of his length. Then he pushes my legs apart and grips his shaft in his fist. "Are you ready?" he asks. I nod and lick my bottom lip. I'm trembling. At first, I think he's going climb on top of me, but he doesn't. Instead, he swoops forward and picks me up before I have time to process what's happening. He presses my back against the wall and impales me on his shaft, and I cry out.

A white light flashes before my eyes and I'm transported somewhere far, far away from the bungalow.

Sara is screaming as wet slapping sounds fill the air. Wes's grunts and hoarse commands follow after, adding to my arousal. I'm floating above my body but unable to see a thing until I can see... stars? A kaleidoscope of colors flashes before me and at first, I'm unsure what I'm looking at. And then I see it: the gold and pink nebula. It's gorgeous and ethereal and so much more amazing than any photograph I've seen.

I reach out to touch it, but then I'm snapped back to the bungalow. Grunts and moans bring me back to reality, and Aiden's intense hazel eyes are boring into me as he pumps in and out of my cunt. His biceps are rigid from holding me in place, and I can make out a thick vein in his neck as sweat runs down the length of it.

"What—what was that?" I moan, and for a split second I don't even recognize my own voice. Aiden slows his thrusts down and laughs.

"Did you see stars, baby?"

I nod. "Is that... normal?"

"It means I'm doing my job right," he murmurs. My breasts bounce in tandem to his movements and he takes a moment to suck on one of the sensitive nipples. I moan as he slides in and out of me, gently this time, giving me a moment to catch my breath. Then he lays me back against the bed on my side. He positions himself behind me and lifts my legs to spear my cunt once again. It takes all my willpower to not disappear into the galaxy of stars again. As nice as that was, I'd rather stay here in the moment with Aiden.

Sara comes from somewhere behind us, her wails growing in volume. Wes pads over to the side of our bed and grins down at me as Aiden pumps in and out of my cunt.

"Hey there, mind if I join?" he asks as he fists his length.

Aiden grunts his approval, but they both wait for me to give the go-ahead. I nod, and Wes is on the bed, sandwiching me between two walls of muscle. I hear the crinkle of plastic and watch as Wes rolls a condom down over the tip of his length, which is bigger than I anticipated. He strokes my cheek with the back of his hand before pressing his mouth against mine. I moan into his mouth and he laughs.

"Are you into anal, Taryn?" he asks.

The casualness of his question almost makes me laugh. Brandon always wanted to do anal, but I never let him, much to his disappointment. I guess just because you spend five years of your life with someone doesn't necessarily mean you want to surrender all of your holes to them. But if there was one person who I trusted with my ass, it was Wes.

"Never tried it," I say as Aiden slows his thrusting down. "Willing to experiment, though."

Sara tosses a bottle of lube over from her bed and Wes catches it in mid-air. The three of them are just so practiced that I can't help but think they probably fuck one another constantly. They're all so in-tune with one another's needs, there's no way that they don't. Wes takes his time applying lube to my other hole as Aiden fucks me slowly, rocking his hips back and forth in a gentle rhythm. Once he's done with the lube, he inserts a finger, and I gasp.

"How's this, princess?" he asks.

I smirk. "Okay, I have to ask. What's with the whole princess thing?"

Wes shrugs. "Oh, just something we've all decided to call you, since you're our princess for the weekend."

"Why is that?" I ask as he fingers my ass. It's taking every ounce of concentration I have left to be able to form coherent sentences. Sweat rolls down my side and Aiden grips my waist in a tight hug, holding me in place.

"Princesses get taken care of and doted on by their servants," Aiden growls into my ear. "And we are at your service, baby."

Wes presses the tip of his cock into my ass as Aiden holds me tighter. I moan as every cell in my body quivers with lust. Aiden begins to pick up the pace with his thrusts again, and Wes begins to pump in and out of my ass with ease. I'm getting fucked by two guys at once. I've seen it done in porn before and thought it looked overwhelming, and it is. It's definitely overwhelming, but not in a bad way.

I scream as the two men pump away in both my holes, and the slaps echo throughout the room.

"Fuck, fuck, fuck!" I yell, and both men laugh. Sara giggles from somewhere behind us, but thanks to Aiden's massive shoulders being in the way, I can't see her. A few seconds later, I'm coming again, and so are Wes and Aiden. They hiss and grunt as they come in spurts, and when they're finished, they pull themselves free from my body.

We lay together in a sweaty heap on the bed for several minutes before both gentlemen extract themselves to dispose of the condoms and clean themselves up. Sara and I cuddle in the bed and luxuriate in the air conditioning, which is working overtime just to cool down the room to a respectable temperature.

"Who's going to be first in the shower?" I ask, not moving from my spot in the bed. Sara nuzzles into the crook of my neck and giggles.

"The shower is big enough for all of us," she whispers in my ear. I shudder as Wes walks out of the bathroom holding a damp towel and dabs at my thighs. They really weren't kidding when they said I was their princess. "We don't need to get up yet, do we?"

I smirk as Wes wipes the sweat away from my stomach. "Nah. I think we're fine here."

The four of us cuddle together as I turn on the news, which is showing a marathon of Con footage, including the parade from earlier that day. Luckily, I don't have any early morning panels to get to because I don't think

I'd make it to any of them even if I did.

"What's on your mind?" Aiden asks as he looks over to catch me staring at the screen in a daze.

"I was just thinking about how this started off as the worst Con ever."

Aiden tugs me against his chest and cradles me like I'm a precious baby bird in need of coddling. A cuddle puddle in the middle of the bed is exactly what I needed after all, I guess.

"And now?" he asks.

I lift one shoulder in a half-shrug. "Probably best Con ever. We'll see." I grin as Sara rests her head on my shoulder. The four of us fall asleep to the sound of the television.

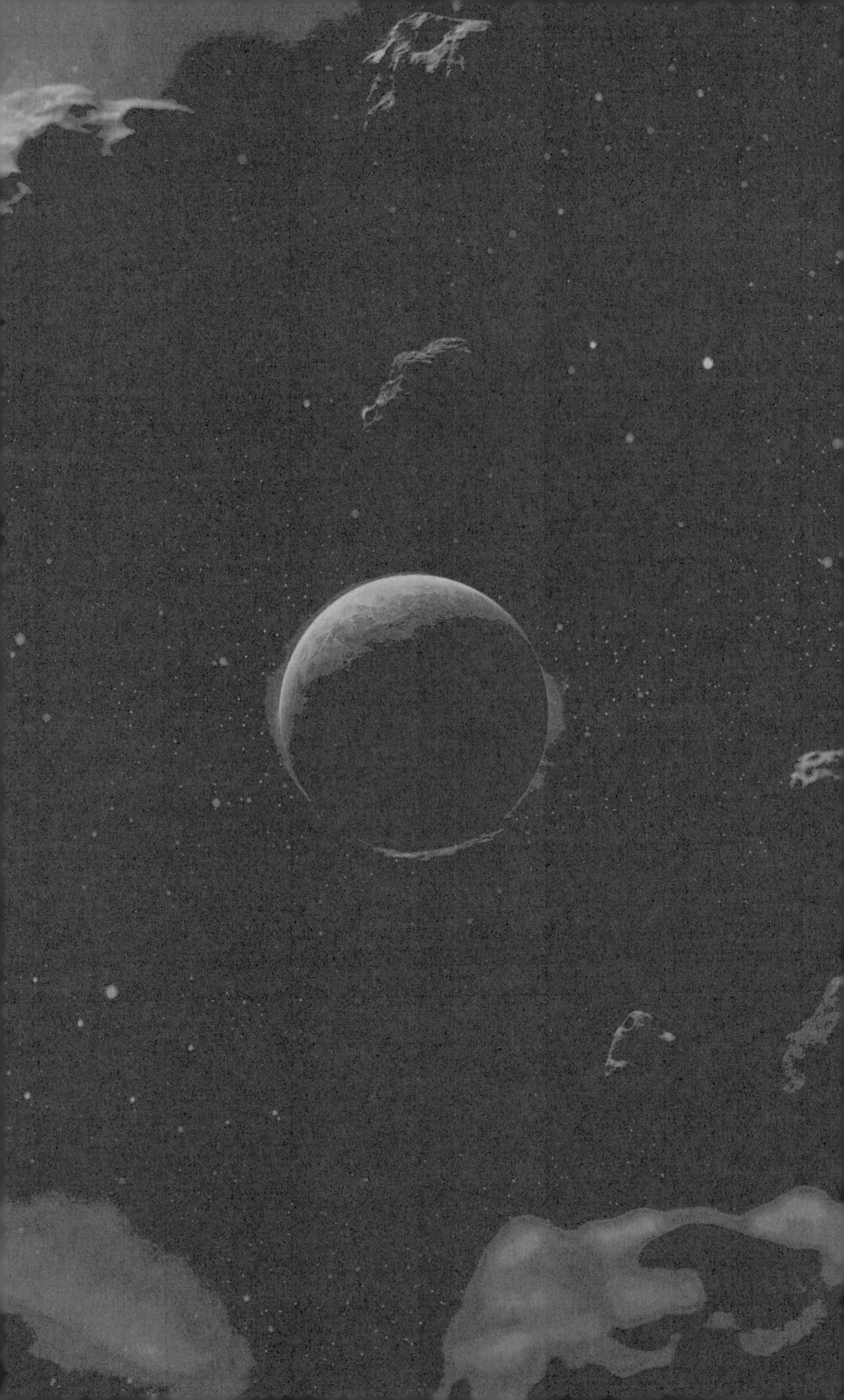

Chapter Five

The weekend goes by in a blitz, and by Sunday evening the four of us are exhausted and ready for a week-long nap. I flop onto my bed face-first while Sara makes herself a cup of coffee with the in-room Coffee Mate.

"So, what are your plans for the rest of the year?" Sara asks as she busies herself with opening up several of the tiny creamer containers. I roll onto my back and stare up at the ceiling as I consider her question. I hadn't really thought about it, and the question gnaws at my insides like a playful puppy going at a bone. I let out a long, exasperated sigh before answering.

"No clue. Brandon was going to a conference in Germany in October. I was supposed to go with him, but… obviously that's out of the question, now," I say bitterly. I was really looking forward to that trip, too. I looked up all the fun touristy things to do online back in July and was totally ready to make the most of the time. I'd be alone during most of the trip. Now I'm realizing I'm more disappointed about missing out on Germany than not being with Brandon anymore. Funny how that works.

"Oh, I'm sorry," she says as she pours herself a cup. I sit up, and she raises the mug in my direction. "Want one? You look like you could use a little pick-me-up. Or would you like me to snuggle you silly instead?"

I swallow hard at her sudden suggestion and my cheeks alight with a scorching heat that spreads to my chest and shoulders. "Just snuggling?"

She smiles and takes a sip from her cup. "It's okay. I'm mostly teasing. Unless your answer is yes, then I'm being totally serious."

Sara is adorable, and today she's dressed in a way that makes her look like a piece of cake. I wonder if she tastes as sweet as she looks. I haven't had a chance to go down on her yet, but there's still time. Sara walks over to the edge of the bed and sits down next to me. Her candy floss pink hair is still in perfect condition even though the weekend was… intense, to say the least, and her lavender peplum top shows off every single one of her delicious curves. I'm not sure what kind of bra she's wearing, but I like it. It presses her breasts up into perfectly round shapes that are begging to be squeezed and teased. I also wouldn't mind getting my lips on them, and I imagine myself licking the blush-hued nipples underneath. We look at one another for several lingering moments and she leans in to press her lips against my cheek. It's chaste, but I blush anyway. I'm not used to such outward displays of affection. Brandon wasn't a big hugger. Now I'm realizing just how much I've been missing out on for the past five years.

"Sorry, I really should have asked first," she says with a sad smile.

"It's okay, I liked it. You're good," I say. Sara gets up to walk into the bathroom. I'm disappointed when she leaves, because it means we probably aren't going to hook up this morning. We'd had so much fun this weekend and were rarely apart for more than ten minutes at a time. We drank, ate at one of the local hibachi grills, and went to so many parties it feels like I'll never get rid of the dark circles under my eyes. I hardly saw Amber this weekend, but not for lack of trying. She met someone the first night of the con and was… well, she was a little distracted. We texted, of course, and had lunch together in the food court twice. She made sure I had an open invitation to spend the weekend with her and her new friend, but I didn't want to be a third wheel. Besides, I had my own company. All was well in the universe for once.

Sara reemerges from the bathroom wearing a tiny black triangle bikini that barely covers the most important bits of her body. She also pulled her hair back into a high ponytail, and she took the time to remove most of her makeup. It's strange to see her without her makeup, but seeing her fresh-faced feels much more intimate.

"I'm going up to the rooftop pool for the party, and you're definitely coming with," she says. Seeing her in her swimsuit is enough to get me into the bathroom to change without a single complaint. One last hurrah before we have to go home, I guess.

I really, really do not want to go home. Sure, there's always next year, but I don't even know where my new friends are from, and we never discussed plans for keeping in touch after the con. My stomach sinks as I tie my blue halter top suit into place around my neck. What if that was the plan all along? Have fun for one long weekend and then leave without even exchanging numbers? What if I never see them again? Am I even allowed to feel sad about this? After all, I had planned on having a quick rebound hookup. Mission accomplished, sure, so then why did it feel so bad? Maybe I'm just not a hookup person. Maybe what I really wanted was… them. All of them, as something more.

Sara knocks lightly on the door, and when I open it, her smile grows as large as her face.

"Wow, missy. You're smokin' hot," she says as she looks me up and down with a lusty gaze. "I mean, unsurprising. I've seen you naked, but something about you in this bikini just hits different."

My halter bikini is the only thing that support my tits comfortably, and I've always been self-conscious about my hips. They're wide, and so is my ass. It's not that I don't love my body, I do, but society doesn't always feel the same way. I've endured plenty of fatphobic comments throughout my life, both from strangers and people who were supposed to be my friends. Even Brandon liked to hint at me spending more time at the gym, even though I was already in there ten hours a week because I love lifting heavy objects. This is just how my body is, and it's nice that Sara appreciates me the way I am.

"Thanks," I say as I tuck my hair behind my ears. "Are Aiden and Wes coming, too?"

She nods. "They're already up there. I got a text from Wes a little while ago that the party is starting to get crowded, so we should head up asap."

I throw on my sheer sarong and flip-flops and head up to the roof with her. Wes wasn't kidding. The party is crammed with people in both regular cosplay and cosplay swimsuits. Wes waves to us from the other side of the pool. Aiden is with him, looking grumpy that so many people are splashing near him. But when he looks up and sees me, all irritation melts away into a smile. When we walk over to drop our stuff off on one of the pool chairs, I can see not only is Aiden smiling, he's blushing something fierce.

"You look nice," he says as he leans against the side of the pool, giving me a sweet view of his biceps. Wes beckons us into the pool, and Sara plunges in feet first. She hisses as the cold water shocks her system, and I smile as I timidly dip one of my toes in over the side. I plop down on my butt and let my legs dangle into the water.

Wes grabs onto one of my calves and pulls. I squeal, and Aiden pushes him away.

"You're not doing yourself any favors just sitting up there like that. You need to jump in and get it over with," Wes says with a mischievous grin. Yeah, he's probably right, but that doesn't mean I have to do it. Aiden shrugs as he hovers close to me, almost protectively.

Eventually, I drop into the water and wince as the ice water stings my skin. It only hurts a little at first, but after a while, the water feels like heaven once the sun comes out from behind the clouds. All four of us lean against the back of the pool's edge as we watch the party-goers do their thing. The Flying Spaghetti Monster is back, and this time they're playing a rousing game of cornhole with a man dressed as Jesus. The irony is too much for me to handle, so I turn to Aiden and smile.

"So, con's almost over, huh?" I say in a lighthearted voice, but inside I'm actually dying a little. Aiden smiles back at me and puts an arm around my shoulder.

"Yeah. It went by fast," he mutters. Wes looks over at Aiden over the top of his sunglasses and frowns.

Abduction Seduction

"Almost time to go back to reality," Wes says.

"Ugh, I hate reality. It's too stressful," Sara says as she throws her arms up in disgust.

"There's something the three of us want to ask you later. In your room," Aiden says. A tingle runs down the length of my spine. I look back at Wes and Sara, who nod along in agreement. I narrow my eyes as I wait for them to drop some clues, but none of them elaborate. Okay, yeah. Definitely concerning, but I'm not running away. Not after the most enjoyable weekend I've had in forever.

"Can we go now?" I ask. Sara laughs and splashes me playfully with cool water.

"No, silly, we just got here. Don't worry, it'll be worth the wait." She winks at me. Aiden shifts beside me, and when I look up to smile at him, he grimaces back.

"Yeah. Hope so," I murmur.

Two hours later, we're all sick of the pool and crowds so we go back downstairs to my room. The air conditioning is bracing, and I dive underneath the duvet of my bed to get warm.

"Where's your roommate, anyway? We haven't seen her the entire weekend. I'm starting to doubt her existence," Sara says as she peers out the window. The view from the room isn't bad. It overlooks the street, and down below all the con-goers look like tiny, colorful jimmies scattered along the pavement.

I let out a deep, contented sigh as I starfish out on the bed. "Amber? Oh, she found a distraction of her own. She's been shacking up with her all weekend. Evidently, she's a local and has a mansion with a pool and jacuzzi. She invited me to come along, but I gave her my blessing to go hook up and have a good time without me."

"That's cool of her, and of you," Sara says. Wes snorts while he starts making himself a cup of coffee. Geez, these three really love their coffee. Not that I blame them. We haven't exactly been sleeping much since we got here.

"Yeah, she's a good friend," I mutter as I close my eyes. Aiden sits on the edge of the bed and looks back at me, like he wants to climb into the bed but doesn't want to invade my personal space. I reach for him with both arms open and claw at the air like a cat making biscuits. He smiles and lays back on his side next to me.

"Are you really attached to Amber?" Sara asks.

I furrow my eyebrows and snort. "That's a weird question. Uh, yeah. She's been my best friend since kindergarten, so I'd say so."

Sara purses her lips. Wes hands her a cup of coffee before slugging his own down, then flops in the chair in the corner. Why do I feel like I'm being interrogated all of a sudden?

"Hm. And what about family?" Sara pivots on her heel. The look on her face is all business, and that scares me.

"Okay, you're starting to worry me here. Why all the grilling?" I ask as I pull my knees into my chest. Aiden rests his hand on top of my knees, but this time, his touch isn't soothing. It's downright worrisome. Wes runs his hand down his face and groans, like the whole situation is frustrating him.

"I told you that we should have just taken her first, then explained everything," he says. My throat tightens.

"What the fuck, you guys?"

I look towards the door. How quickly can I run out of here before one of them snatches me? Would I even make it to the doorway? Doubt creeps in as I plan my escape route. There's nowhere I can run or hide. I guess I could lock myself in the bathroom if I can make it that far, but--

"Go ahead, tell her. You said you trust her, and we agreed with you."

Aiden clears his throat and runs his fingers across his stubble.

"Taryn, the moment I met you, I knew you were special," he begins. Oh my god, is he about to propose? That's too weird. No, no, please don't be a proposal, please don't be a proposal. "And when we received the sample of your blood, my feelings about you were confirmed. You're the one we've been looking for."

My fear is replaced with confusion as my eyebrows slam together. "I'm sorry, what?"

"Your blood type. They told you that you were AB Negative, correct?" Aiden asks. I tilt my head. This isn't getting any clearer.

"Yeah. That's what they told me," I say, annoyance creeping into my words. "What does that have to do with anything?"

Sara swallows hard and sits down in the chair in the corner of the room. "Taryn, we're not from around here."

"Yeah, that much I knew. But you never told me where you're all from," I say. Aside from feeling frightened that I've gotten myself into some sort of human trafficking situation, I'm also just pissed off. I've already been heartbroken once this weekend, and I don't know how I'm going to drive back home alone sixteen hours with another scar on my heart. Aiden reaches underneath the blankets and searches for my hand. I let him take it. As Wes drinks from his coffee cup, he points up at the ceiling with his index finger.

"What's that supposed to mean? Could you please use your words? And what did Wes mean by 'taking me'? Take me where? Are you trying to kidnap me?" I ask, unable to keep the panic from my voice.

"We're from up there," Wes says, almost bored-sounding as he drains his cup.

"You're saying you're from up north? Enough with the bullshit already. We've been through enough together this weekend that I'd like to think you could trust me with knowing where you live!"

"We're from another planet," Wes says dryly.

His words don't even register until several moments later. Is he fucking with me right now? This 'we're a bunch of aliens' shit again? It's not cute or clever to have me on the hook like this, and I'm shuffling out of the bed when Aiden lifts my hand and kisses the back of it.

"Taryn, we're from another star system similar to yours. We left our home world in search of a cure for a very serious illness that has been causing an extinction-level event. Your blood holds the key to the medicines we're trying to craft that will fight this disease and save our people," Sara says, her voice calm and even. She watches me carefully, like I'm a spooked cat ready to bolt out the door at any second. And she's right, I am.

"Let's just say I believe you, which I don't. Because that would be ridiculous," I say indignantly.

Sara's face fell. Either I disappointed her that her little ruse wasn't working, or she was disappointed because she was telling the truth and I was laughing in her face.

"I figured you, of all people, would be open-minded enough to at least entertain the idea that we exist. That other worlds exist, Taryn," she said, her voice wavering.

I place my feet on the ground and look back at the door again. I really want to get the hell out of here, but a part of me is curious just how far they're going to go with this.

"Why? You barely know anything about me."

Aiden places his hand on my shoulder, and I jerk away.

"For starters, your profession. You're a cryptozoologist, right?" Sara asks. I nod. "You have a vlog with five-hundred thousand subscribers just about cryptids."

I roll my eyes. "Yes. That's true, but the first thing you should know about me is that I am forever and always a skeptic. I dig for the truth. I don't go onto my channel and just hype up every fuzzy phone vid I come across."

Sara paces in front of the window while Wes leans back in the chair. No one says anything for a long, tense moment. If I'm going to leave, now seems to be my chance. I slide off the bed and head to the dresser where I left my dress.

"I think we should just show her. This is going to take too long and humans need concrete proof," Wes says as I gather up my belongings. I turn around to see Aiden unzipping his pants. They slip over his hip bones onto the floor in a crumpled pile.

"Wait, what are you—"

Sara holds up her finger, silencing me. Wes gets up from the chair and heads into the bathroom and closes the door behind him. My heart slams into my throat as my fight-or-flight instincts kick in, and they're telling me to run. Run and don't look back. But my feet won't move. It's like I've lost control over my limbs, no matter how badly I want to sprint out of here.

"Just give him a sec, Taryn," Sara murmurs.

"A second for what?"

"Can you both just… not say anything? I'm sorry, I don't mean to be rude, but could you please turn around, Taryn?" Aiden asks. I gape at him like his hair's suddenly on fire. The audacity, asking me to turn around. Why? So he can knock me out? Put a bag over my head? I don't move.

"Please?" he implores sweetly. "I promise, we're not going to hurt you. I would never hurt you, Taryn. Not ever."

I don't know what compels me to believe him, but I turn around. He mutters a quick 'thank you,' and the sound of his shirt hitting the floor is the only other noise in the room. I have no idea what Wes is doing in the bathroom, and I don't really want to know.

"You can turn back around now. Just don't panic, okay? Don't scream," Aiden says. I blink. Did he just…? Yeah. I'm not imagining things. His voice was definitely just inside of my head, like some sort of telepathy. My heart beats in my ears now, drowning out the sound of Aiden's voice as he asks me to turn around. Then I notice my hands. They're trembling. Actually, my entire body is trembling, like it just knows that whatever I'm going to see when I turn around isn't going to be pleasant.

"It's okay, Taryn. Just turn around," Sara says, her voice firm but gentle. "Just remember, you're not in any danger."

This whole situation is fucked, but it's not likely to get any better unless I turn around. With my heart pounding in my veins, I finally turn around and come face to face with a monster. A real flesh and blood monster. I let out a blood-curdling scream and drop to my knees.

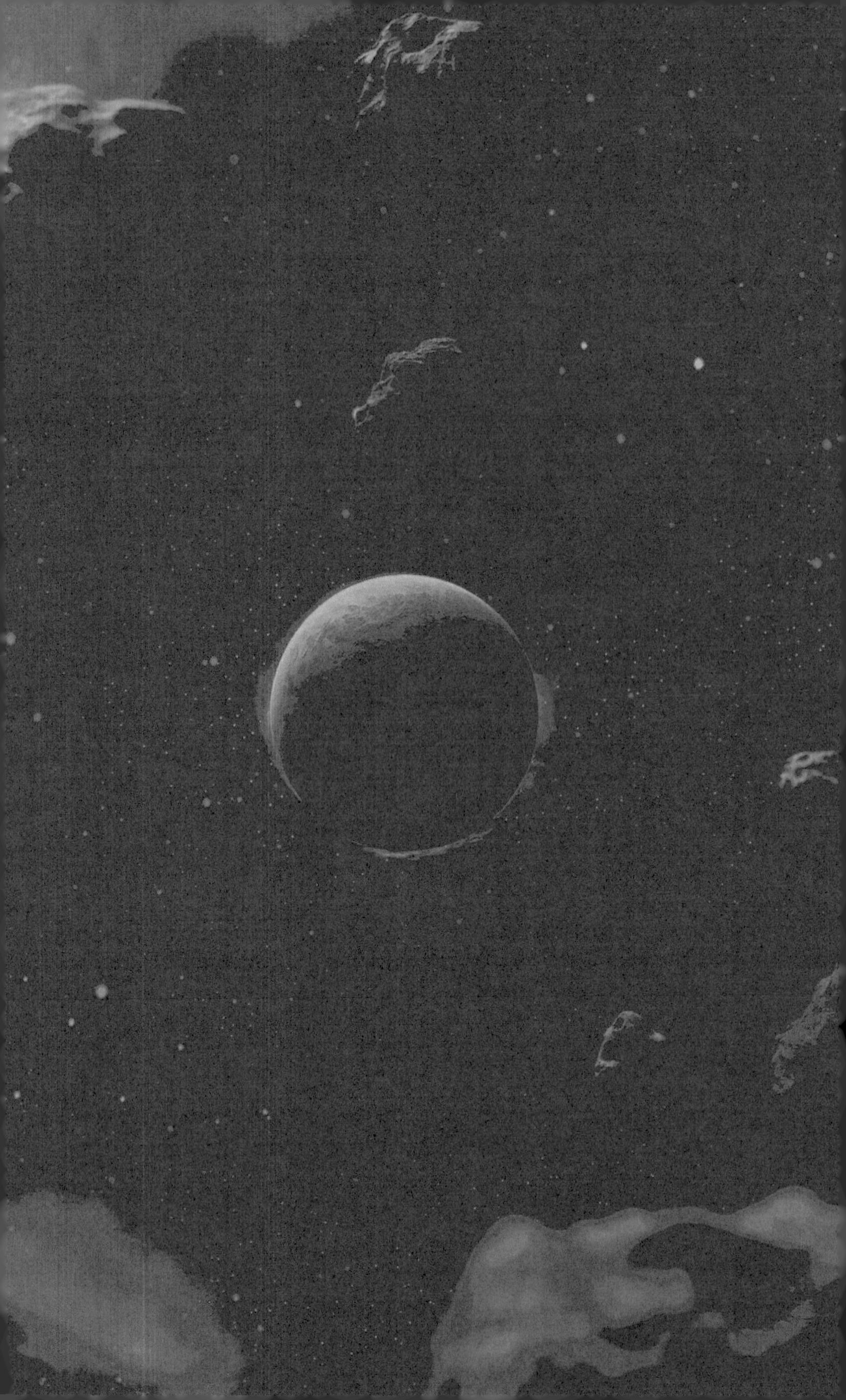

Chapter Six

The creature's eyes are enormous, almond-shaped morasses that stare back at me, unblinking. The kind of eyes you'd find on a bug, or… or a gray. As in, one of the gray aliens, a subtype of alien species made popular by films and television. Meeting one face to face never even occurred to me. I mean, I'm a believer, of course I am, but I assumed actual aliens wouldn't look like anything from the movies. I feel woozy and the room spins in a violent swirl of color. Sara yells something, but I can't hear her. The room takes on the appearance of an oil spill, all rainbow-hued and watery. Then the light dims to a muted brown color until I can no longer see anything at all. The voices of my friends float far, far away until only darkness remains.

By the time I wake up, it's pitch black inside the room, save for the moonlight that trickles in through the curtains. I groan from the pressure behind my eyes, rub them, and strain as I push myself into a sitting position. It's a long minute before I finally remember what happened to me, and my pulse races as I look around the room. Sara is sitting next to me on the bed, offering a glass of water. I take it and mumble my thanks before tipping the lukewarm tap water down my throat.

She frowns and looks around the room, like she isn't sure what to say, so she says nothing at all.

"Where's… wait, where is Aiden? Is he okay? Did something happen to his face?" I ask as I rub my head. I try to take another sip of water, but my stomach gurgles in protest. Okay, nope. Don't feel like vomiting all over the fancy hotel comforter.

"Do you not remember what happened?" she asks quietly.

I narrow my eyes as I try to conjure the blurry memories that swirl inside my head. Which, by the way, feels like it just got kicked by a horse.

"Not really. I remember…"

The glass in my hand slips. Before it can fall onto the comforter, Sara snatches it mid-air. I stare at her, wide eyed in bewilderment.

"Holy fuck, how did you grab that so fast? Good catch."

Sara sets the glass down on the nightstand on her side of the bed and puts an arm around my shoulder.

"It's okay. It was a lot. We didn't want to introduce ourselves to you this way. The plan was always just to give you a sedative, take you with us, then bring you back. No harm, no foul."

I furrow my brow. "What are you talking about? So, you *were* planning on kidnapping me?"

She doesn't answer, which is enough for me. I leap to my feet and bolt for the front door. The bathroom door swings open, and a man rushes forward to grab me. No. Not a man—at least not a human one. An alien. An enormous, broad-shoulder gray alien with bug-eyes grabs my arms and forces them down to my sides. I let out a blood-curdling shriek.

"No! Get off of me! Get off!" I cry, but the more I resist, the harder the alien presses me to his chest.

"Wes, stop it!" Sara screams. "You're scaring her! We talked about this!"

The alien—Wes?—releases my arms, but he doesn't let me get anywhere near the door. His big body blocks my path. I can't stand to look at his face. It's too terrifying. Sara grabs onto my hand and tugs me back towards the bed, and I don't offer any resistance this time.

"I'm sorry, Taryn," she mumbles. I sit down on the edge of the bed and stare at the wall. None of this is real. They must have given me something before I blacked out, but I don't remember drinking anything.

"Did you drug me?" I ask. The lightheadedness is coming back, and the nausea in my stomach won't let up.

Sara shakes her head, her pink hair bouncing almost comically on her shoulders.

"No, sweetheart. No, we would never. I'm so sorry. We thought you'd be a lot… calmer about this."

"Calmer about this?" I repeat, looking up at her with watery eyes. I don't even know what any of 'this' is. Wes walks into the room and I scramble back on the bed in a panic. Nothing about the way he moves looks fake. It's not a costume. I'm operating on sheer instinct, and it's telling me that Wes is an alien. A gray alien.

"Where's Aiden?" I demand.

Sara shoots me a despondent look and bites her bottom lip. "He left for the ship after he saw your reaction. I think he's hurt."

I snort. "He's *what?*"

The thought of Aiden's feelings being hurt after that sort of revelation blows my mind. What was I supposed to do? Squeal with delight and jump up and down for joy!?

"Yeah, well. You kind of passed out when you looked at him." Wes's voice blasts in my mind as if I had just tuned into a broadcast on the radio. I flinch and rub my temples.

"Don't yell, please," I say, wincing.

"I'm not yelling. Taryn, we need you to come with us. Either you come with us willingly, or I'm taking you."

Sara shoots Wes a look of pure rage. "No, we're not. Either she comes willingly or not at all."

"But we need her! We have literally one job! Get the girl back home. Offer our people her blood as a cure. Done."

Wes's admission is all the proof I need to send me trying for the door again. He gives chase, but when Sara screams for him to stop, he doesn't pursue me into the hallway. I feel like I'm going to pass out or vomit, or both. I can't. Not until I've gotten to safety. I race past the long hallway until I find the elevators and slam my palm on the button. I know it never works, but I can't keep myself from pressing the button until my fingers start to cramp.

"Come on, come on, come on! Hurry up," I whine.

The doors open, and I push past a couple of gentlemen in suits to get inside the lift. When the doors finally close, I let out a long sigh of relief.

I'm safe.

Now, all I need to do is get to reception and tell them what happened. Call the police. Get the fuck out of here.

I can't believe this is happening.

I can't believe that the aliens are actually real. They're here, and they want *me*. Me, of all people. Why not someone better suited for this? Like Ethan Godwick, for crying out loud? He's actually somebody in the paranormal community! I'm just a nobody with a vlog that hardly anyone cares about anymore. I suck in a breath impatiently as the elevator stops from floor to floor. Every time the doors creak open, my heart slams into my chest. A couple women in glamorous, rhinestone dresses get on once the lift hits the second floor and they barely look at me.

I can't believe I slept with them. All three of them!

It was the hottest sex I've ever had in my life. And that one orgasm? Holy shit. But still… they lied to me.

Then a memory emerges from the other day in the lobby. Sara tried to tell me the truth, that they were aliens from another planet. At the time, I didn't believe her. But she was trying to tell me and I didn't believe her, not even for a second.

The elevator dings as it hits the lobby. The women disembark, and I follow behind them. I stuff my hands into the pockets of my dress and make a beeline for the front door, skipping reception. What could I possibly say to them? That there are aliens upstairs on the tenth floor? They won't believe me, and there's even a good chance they aren't in the room anymore. The staff will just think I'm drunk, or playing a Chimera Con prank.

Part of me feels a little guilty, but I'm not sure why.

Abduction Seduction

Wes mentioned something about needing my blood because their people were dying. If that's true, then my running away quite possibly just doomed an entire alien species. I take a cab to one of the conference buildings Amber is supposed to be in, but when I get there, she's nowhere to be found. I pull out my phone to call her, but notice a missed text from earlier. It was Amber. She texted to let me know she was staying a little longer with her new friend and that I shouldn't wait for her. Well, looks like I'll be making the trip back up to Philly on my own, then.

All of my stuff is still back in my hotel room, so I have to go back. It's risky, but after an hour, I finally return to the hotel and head up to my room. Luckily, there's no sign of the trio. I flop onto the bed, not even bothering to remove my makeup. It's been that sort of day, and I process stressful situations slower than the average person. Within seconds of my head hitting the pillow, I fall fast asleep.

When I get up the next morning, I don't even bother with caffeine before I grab my things, checkout, and get into my car. I look at myself in the rearview mirror and cringe. My mascara is smeared across my cheeks, along with the plum eyeshadow I wore the night before. I really should have taken thirty seconds to wash my face last night. No wonder the woman at the reception desk kept staring at me.

Approximately nine hours later, I'm somewhere outside of Roanoke, Virginia. Driving alone has been lonely without Amber's constant chatter and endless stream of podcasts to keep me entertained. We were making our way through season one of *Welcome to Nightvale*, and I miss the dulcet tones from Cecil's voice coming out of my speakers. I hope Amber is doing okay. She has to be doing better than I am right now. When I pull off at a service stop to grab some gas, I take out my phone to text her, then stop myself when I realize there's another number in here.

It's Aiden's.

I don't remember putting his number in here. He has a phone? I didn't know that. I never saw him use one. But... how? How does an alien even have cell service? And if I called or texted him right now, would he get my messages? I nibble my bottom lip as I stare at his name underneath the soft glow of the lights from the station. Out of the corner of my eye, I catch a glimmer of yellow light flash past. Assuming it's another car pulling in for gas, I don't bother to look up.

Then I hear it.

The humming.

It's subtle, but it's there.

For a split second, I forget what I was doing. The phone in my hand buzzes gently, and Aiden's name pops up on the screen.

"What the hell?" I murmur to myself, then put the phone to my ear. "Hello? Aiden?"

The voice on the other end is scratchy, like a radio signal too weak to come in clearly.

"Hello?"

There's no response, and the call drops. I step out of my car and look around. Nowhere around. It's a ghost town. I don't even see anyone inside at the cash register inside the shop. My breathing quickens as I walk around the gas station in search of clues. If those three plan on popping out and abducting me after all, then they better show themselves or else I'm going to give them a piece of my mind for scaring the shit out of me twice in the span of twenty-four hours.

"Hello?" I ask the darkness at the edge of the lot. Only the wind responds. Not even the crickets are chirping. The stillness is deeply unsettling, the sort of thing I've only seen in movies right before—

"I couldn't leave before saying goodbye," a voice rings in my mind, clear as a bell. At first, I don't recognize it. It doesn't even sound human. Then the voice speaks again, this time, only my name. "Taryn."

The voice is deep and masculine. Aiden.

"Where are you?" I ask as I pivot on my heel. I don't see him anywhere.

"Out in the field with the ship. I didn't want to frighten you again with my appearance. But I just wanted to say… I never meant to scare you, Taryn."

I place my hands on my hips, indignant. There's no way I want him to see how terrified I am at this very moment. "Well, you did a real bang-up job with that. Wes told me everything," I say.

I wrap my arms around myself as the wind blows against my cheeks. Despite it being early September, the breeze carries the faintest promise of autumn along with it.

"Not everything. And he was wrong to threaten you. We weren't going to kidnap you. That was never the plan."

I want to believe him, I really do. But it's hard to trust someone whose entire identity was obfuscated for the greater part of the weekend. They lied to me. After everything that happened between me and Brandon, and then this? I'm tired.

As if reading my mind, Aiden says, "I know it's inappropriate, asking you to trust my word on that, after everything that happened this weekend. I do apologize for everything. That's all I wanted to say, Taryn. That, and I'll miss you."

My throat tightens. This isn't the right thing to do, letting things end like this. I mean, yeah, I'm pretty ticked off with all three of them right now, but I'm also… curious? I'm a cryptozoologist no matter what happens in my personal life, and a large part of me craves answers. I've been to dozens of panels held by people who claimed to be alien abductees. Some were credible, others not so much. This could be the first and only chance I get to uncover the truth about alien lifeforms.

"Wait," I say, hoping I'm not too late. "What did you mean when you said Wes didn't tell me everything?"

For a second, I'm afraid Aiden and the others already took off. But the humming in the distance is steady and constant. They're still there, probably trying to figure out how much they want (or can) tell me.

"I'd be happy to fill you in. Perhaps over a coffee?" Aiden says.

I smirk. Coffee. Of course, it's coffee. They never drink anything else.

"Sure," I say, trying to hide the amusement from my voice.

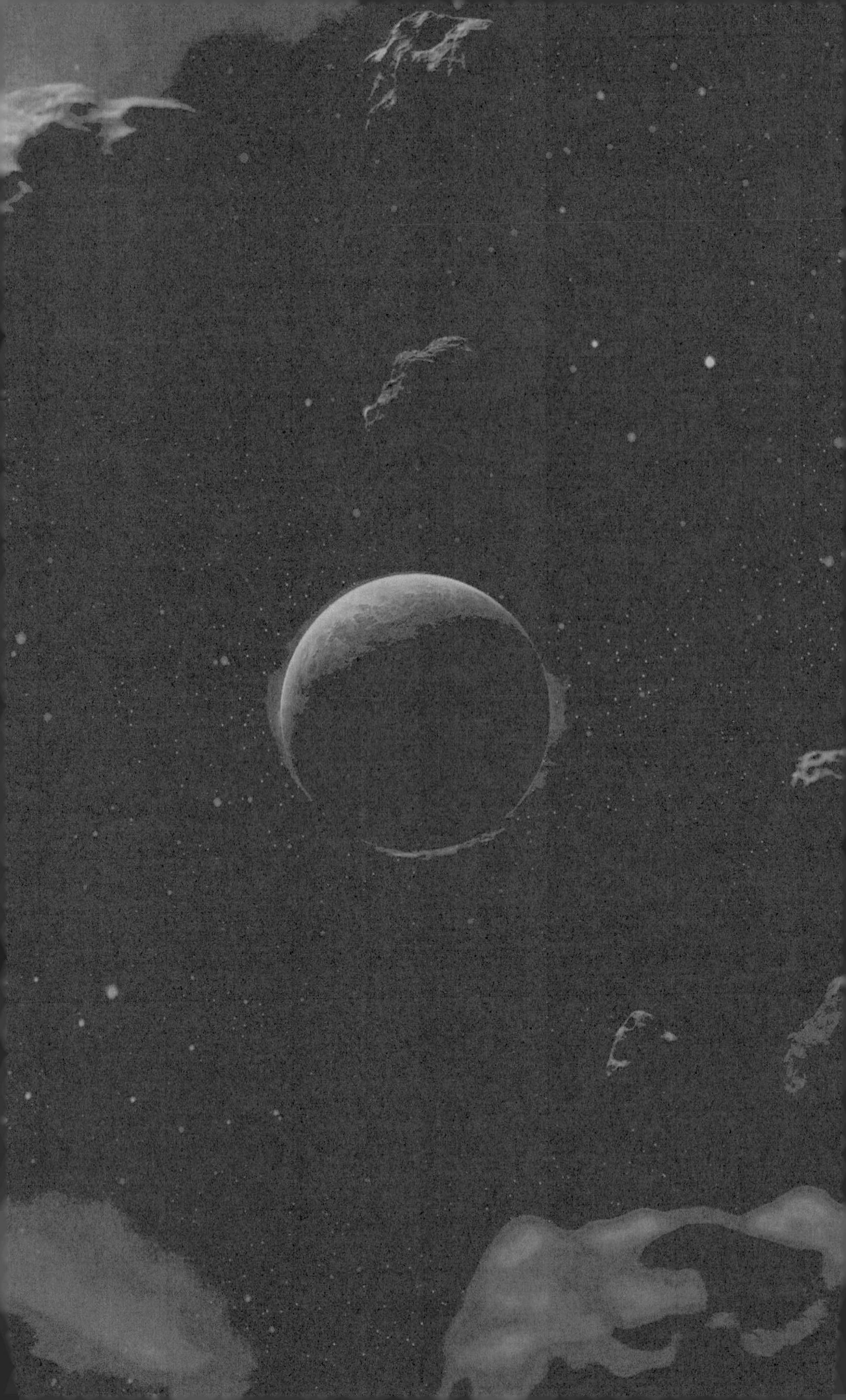

Chapter Seven

The only place to grab a coffee on I-95 at this hour is Sheetz. The neon glow of the signage greets me when I pull into the near-empty parking lot. Good. Fewer people to nose into my business. I step out of the car, lock it, and lean against the door as I wait for… for what, exactly? For Aiden to show up in his spaceship? I have no idea what I'm doing here. I could just be hallucinating this entire night, for all I know. At least this Sheetz has a serviceable gas station, unlike the last place I stopped at. I'm still not even sure if that was due to the spaceship running interference, or something else. It's too creepy to contemplate.

"Taryn," Aiden's voice breaks into my thoughts, but this time, it's not telepathically. He's standing by the door to the Sheetz as his human self, waiting.

"Hey," I say as I step up onto the curb. "Are you alone?"

He nods and pulls the door open to the store. "For now. Wes and Sara are back at the—well, they're waiting."

We step inside and order our coffees in silence. The young woman behind the cash register can't seem to keep her eyes off of Aiden. I don't blame her. He's gorgeous, but if only she knew what he really was. I bet she'd run off screaming into the night, never to be heard from ever again. I notice Aiden doesn't put anything in his coffee. No creamer, no sugar. Sheetz coffee is rough without any additions, and I'm not shy about pouring some pumpkin spice creamer into mine.

We take our coffees back out to my car and sit on the hood to stare up at the stars.

"I can't apologize enough," Aiden says after taking a sip of his coffee.

"I know." I'm not sure what else to say.

"I understand you probably weren't expecting any of this."

I snort. Yeah. Understatement of the year. Does anyone actually expect aliens to show up at a fan con? People dressed as aliens, yes. Real, live aliens? Not so much.

"You could say that. I also wasn't expecting to get dumped over a text message, either. I wasn't expecting to hook up with not only one, but three hot aliens who—"

"You think we're hot?" Aiden looks at me, his lips curled into a small smile. I roll my eyes.

"Kind of missing the point here."

He takes another sip of his coffee and sighs. "You're right. You're absolutely right, and I'm sorry. Again. I would at least like to tell you everything, truthfully this time, so you can make up your mind about us. If you decide after I tell you the truth that you would rather get into your car and go home, we won't stop you. I promise."

I look down at my cup of coffee and frown as the steam billows into my face. "Sure."

The least I can do is hear him out, I guess.

"We traveled to your planet a couple of weeks ago. And in case you're wondering," he says as he gives me a pointed look, "we travel between wormholes, not hyperspace like your movies portray."

I swallow the lump in my throat and nod for him to continue.

"We came here because our..." he pauses for a moment as he searches for the appropriate word, "...government sent us to find a cure for a serious illness that has been killing our people in the thousands."

"What illness? Does it have a name?" I ask.

"We call it The Wasting. Well, actually we call it something else in our tongue, but it would translate roughly to The Wasting in yours. It causes a person to become so lethargic they're unable to move, eat, sleep, or drink until eventually they perish."

"And it's killing thousands of you? That doesn't sound like very many, although killing even one person is too many," I say. I don't mean to be insensitive, but there are billions of humans. I doubt anyone would bat an eyelash on earth if only a few thousand people succumbed to such a thing.

"There's only a million of us, so yes. It's a big deal," he says.

I nod and finish the rest of my coffee, then set the empty cup down on the hood next to my thigh. When I look down at his hands, I notice they're trembling. He's scared. Unconsciously, I place my hand over his to comfort him. Aiden flashes me a look of surprise, then stares down at our hands. Our fingers intertwine as he takes a slow, steadying breath.

"Our government… they wanted us to come here, find a willing donor, and bring them back with us. We had no issues with our assignment. We prepared for this exact scenario. Years of training. Years of mentally preparing ourselves for the eventuality that we would be sent to another place outside our galaxy for a greater purpose. What we weren't prepared for was meeting a sentient species. And we definitely didn't expect to find a human such as yourself with the blood we needed."

I furrow my brow as I listen. There are so many questions on the tip of my tongue, but I don't want to interrupt him. Not when he's speaking so freely.

"And I guess… when we met you, we weren't expecting to get so… attached."

I raise an eyebrow. "Attached?"

He nods. "Mm. We, uh, hijacked the blood drive after our trips to the nearby hospitals proved fruitless. It was our last ditch effort for this area before we'd move on."

"What do you mean, hijacked?" I ask, bristling at his choice of words. "Did you do something to those people?"

He winces. "We didn't hurt them, if that's what you're wondering. But… yes, we did abduct them at night and insert chips into their brains to override some of their memories so we could identify potential willing donors when we found someone with your blood type."

I inhale sharply. Okay, I should have expected as much. That would explain why they were acting so strangely at the blood drive.

"That's pretty fucked up, Aiden. You can't just go around inserting chips into people's brains like that without their consent."

He nods, as though expecting my response.

"I know. We wouldn't have done that if we weren't so desperate. But your blood type is rare. Your hospitals… they don't have enough of it. If only we needed type O blood, all our problems would have been solved ages ago," he says sadly as he hangs his head. Either he's a fantastic actor, or he truly is remorseful.

"Right. So, why not just take what I gave you and go back with it, then?" I ask as I pull my hand away. He doesn't try to take my hand back, and he shuffles a couple inches away from me. I appreciate that he's giving me space.

"We need a live donor to go through the wormhole, since we can't store it properly on the ship. It doesn't survive the trip once it's outside of the body. Our scientists aren't entirely sure why. We need the source, and going from hospital to hospital in search of a donor is taking too much time. Wes suggested we take you back with us. While Sara and I agree that would be the easiest thing, it's not the most ethical."

I toss my head back in a bark of laughter. Aiden flinches. "You don't say! No shit, it's not ethical! It's abduction!"

Aiden's shoulders slump forward as he wilts. "I know," he says in a small voice. "Which is why we're not going to do that. We're going to try to find a willing donor elsewhere. Access the Red Cross's database, try to find a willing donor that way. We never wanted to hurt you, though I know we did when we lied. We really do care for you."

Searching for a willing donor could take ages.

His people are dying.

If the roles were reversed, would I be able to let the cure I so desperately needed walk out the door?

No. Probably not.

Aiden looks up at the stars again, and I can see his eyes are glassy with the appearance of unshed tears. He's hurting.

It looks like I have a choice to make. Either I can get back into my car and go home, like he said. I can try to forget any of this ever happened and move on with my life, or I can go with him and help his people. It's not much of a choice. I have to do this. No, I want to do this.

"I'll go with you," I say. His eyes widen as he looks down at me, too stunned to speak. "I'll go with you," I repeat, more firmly this time.

"Taryn, are you sure? We understand we're asking a lot of you," he says, his voice wavering. "You don't have to do anything you don't want to do. I didn't tell you any of this for sympathy points, if that's what you're thinking."

I shake my head. "No, I'm not thinking that. I'm thinking it's the right thing to do, and also... I like you. All three of you. Although I am still pretty pissed off at Wes right now."

He nods. "Understandable. I'll be sure to have a chat with him and, and—"

"No, it's fine. Just..." I lift my hands to his face and caress his cheeks. Aiden's skin is warm to the touch, much warmer than mine. He runs hot, which is perfect because my hands are always cold no matter the season. "Just take me back to your ship and we'll take things from there, okay?"

Tears slip from Aiden's eyes, and he nuzzles my hands. "Thank you. Thank you, thank you. You have no idea what this means to me. To us. To my people."

I don't. Not really, but I can imagine. The relief, love, and overwhelming gratitude in his eyes says enough. I'm doing the right thing. I have to believe that.

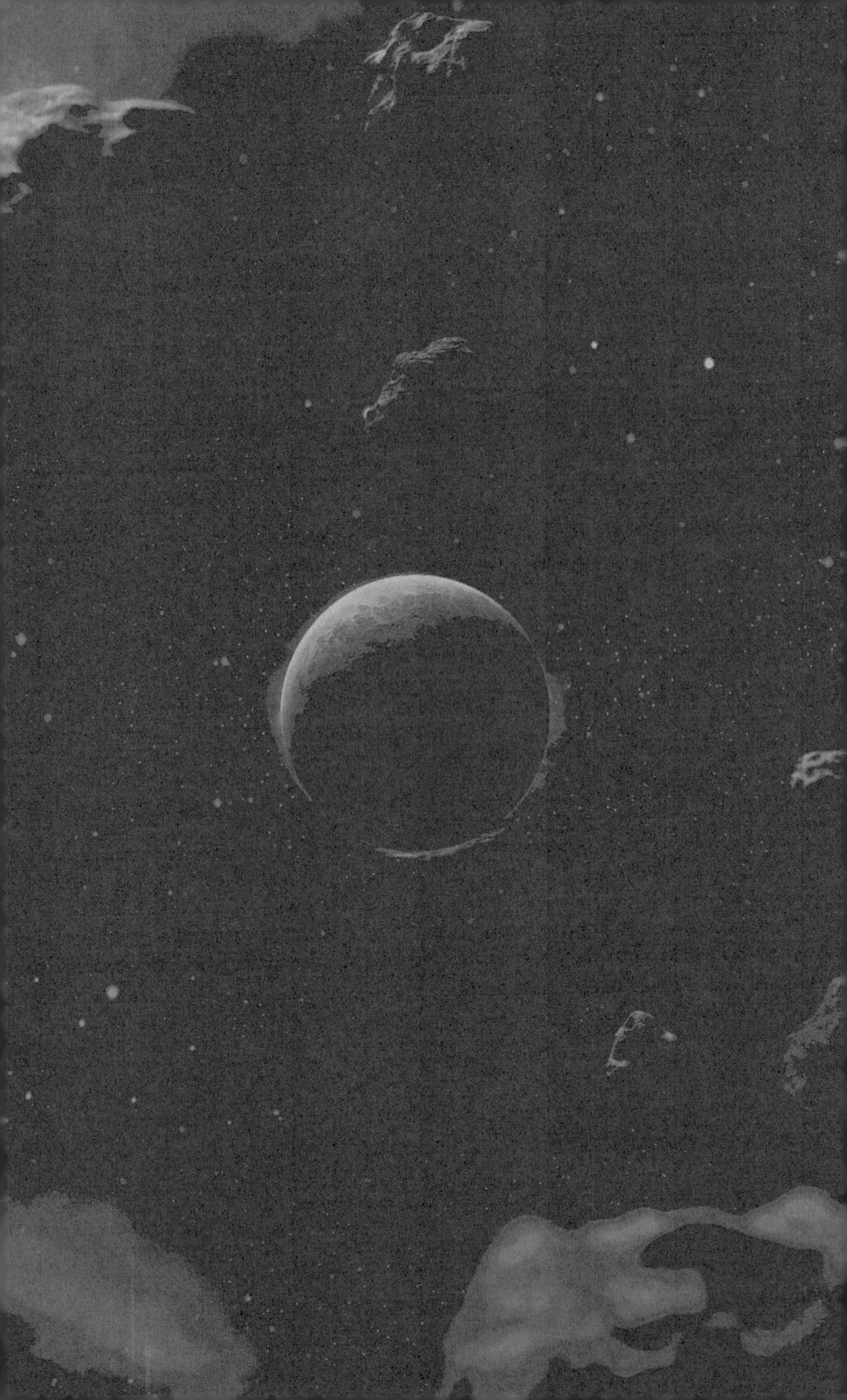

Chapter Eight

The ship looks like a giant platinum football and sits in the middle of a thicket of trees. Aiden waits patiently as I walk the perimeter around the ship, marveling at its beauty. It's so retro looking, I can't help but laugh. I clap a hand over my mouth as I continue to gape in awe, like my brain hasn't fully processed what it's seeing yet.

"Well, shit. Very *Flight-of-the-Navigator*. I like it," I say.

He crosses his arms in front of his chest and frowns. "What is that? Is that another movie reference? I haven't seen all that many, just to warn you. Sara is the movie lover around here."

I snicker. "Yeah. But it's from the eighties and I don't think it was very popular, so, fair enough. I have so many books depicting the ships as silver saucers and footballs. I guess we weren't too far off, huh?"

He shakes his head. "It's because we've been in contact with your species for a long, long time. The eyewitness accounts and testimonies of those abducted were correct. It's just that no one believed them, or they were silenced. Come, we should let Sara and Wes know you're coming with us."

As Aiden steps towards the ship, I'm surprised when the platinum exterior melts to form a ramp leading up to a doorway that wasn't there before. I follow him up the ramp, noting the low hum of the ship. It's the same hum from the gas station. I wasn't hearing things, after all.

The interior of the ship isn't nearly as impressive as its exterior. The walls are completely white, and the floors are a gray rubber-like texture. I don't detect any odd smells, either, which I'm both relieved and disappointed by. If I'm going to go flying around in an alien spacecraft, I was hoping for a little more… well, just more? I don't know what I was expecting, but a dentist's treatment room was not it.

"You're sure you're okay with this?" Aiden asks as he takes my hand in his. He rubs my palm with his thumb, and I can't help but smile.

"I said I would, so I'm going to try."

I don't touch anything other than Aiden's hand as he leads me down a narrow hallway and into a room with four beds inside. The linens are crisp and white, except for the gray pillows and the familiar painting of a galaxy above the white headboard. Okay, if the outside of the ship reminded me of *Flight of the Navigator*, the inside is giving me *Space Odyssey* vibes.

"I was being honest when I said I enjoyed the art as much as you did," he says, and walks over to the bed to pat the mattress. "You may rest here for as long as you like. We're well concealed out here, so there is no rush to leave Earth. We can wait as long as you need to. In case you change your mind, that is."

He's still giving me an out. I appreciate his consideration, but if I wait any longer, there's a chance I'll wuss out and doom his entire planet. No, we need to leave as soon as possible. I sit down on the bed, noting the softness of the mattress and blankets, and kick off my boots. "Thanks, but I think we should get going. Is Sara around?"

Aiden shoves his hands into his jeans pockets and nods. "She's here. So is Wes. He's in the cockpit getting things set up while Sara runs some diagnostic tests. She's our engineer."

"Awesome. Fellow lady in STEM. I can appreciate that."

Aiden tilts his head as he looks at me with a quizzical expression.

"Never mind. Yeah, I'd like to see her."

He starts to leave the room before turning around once he reaches the doorway.

"I know you're angry with him, and what you feel is valid. But I do think you and Wes should talk at some point. He's been beating himself up for the way he treated you earlier."

I let go of a long sigh and press my back against the pillow. "Good. He should feel bad. I'll speak with him. Just... not now. I'm not ready."

"Fair. I'll go let them know you're here, at least."

Aiden leaves the room, giving me time to process my situation. I hope no one finds my car at the edge of the woods. I tried to move it somewhere inconspicuous, but it's going to look really suspicious if someone comes across it out there. I also hope that the planet I'm visiting has a change of clothing, because I didn't exactly have time to pack aside from the bag I already had with me in the car. Most of those clothes were already dirty. My cabin is completely devoid of anything I can entertain myself with, so I'm stuck thinking so much I end up making myself nauseous.

"Taryn?" A familiar voice chirps my name from the doorway. I look up to see Sara standing there. Except... she's not Sara. Not really. Not in the way I remember her.

The alabaster woman standing in the doorway is at least seven feet tall, with angular features that give her a chiseled, stone-like appearance. Her neck reminds me of a giraffe's, slender and elongated. She's also completely bald. Sara takes a few steps into the room, slowly, as though she's afraid she might startle me into fleeing. Where would I even go? I'm trapped in here.

"Sara?" I squeak. The woman nods.

"Yes," she says. When Sara speaks, it's not telepathically. Her lips, while thin, aren't just for show. "This must be confusing."

I shrug. "A little, but it's alright. I take it you aren't the same species."

She shakes her head. "No."

When she reaches to touch my cheek, I don't pull away. Even in this form, she's elegant and breathtakingly gorgeous. I'm not quite sure what that says about me, that I find this form so alluring, but that's something to ponder later.

"Aiden and Wes are shapeshifters. I, on the other hand, can only take on the human disguise with the help of technology." She lifts her rail-thin arm up and waves it around, showing off the silver bangle around her wrist. "I normally keep it in my pocket. Attracts less attention that way."

"Shapeshifters? So, they aren't grays?" I ask as I pat the space next to my thigh. "You can sit, Sara."

She sits down next to me, and I have to lean back in order to see her face.

"No, they aren't… what did you call them? Grays? That's not a very creative name."

I laugh. "I know, but I didn't exactly come up with it. It's just an old term for gray, big-eyed aliens we put into our movies all the time."

She nods. "I see. No, they're…" Sara stops, and her brilliant, crystal-blue eyes turn glassy. "Sorry, that was Wes. He was asking if we were ready to leave."

My stomach lurches. "I… yeah. I guess so. If not now, then when, right?"

Sara pats my head. Her hands are long, flat, and tipped with claws that look more like knives than fingernails.

"Good. I would lie down if I were you. The sensation can feel like you're being pulled apart, but it only lasts around thirty seconds."

Oh, god. Pulled apart? What have I gotten myself into? She seems to notice the fear on my face and offers me a small smile.

"Really, it's not so bad. Don't worry, I only warned you so you didn't try to walk around your cabin and tip over!"

I really, really don't want to be left alone in the cabin while all of this is going on. I reach for her arm as she starts to leave. "Wait. Can't you stay with me? Please?"

Sara regards me sadly. "I'm sorry, sweetheart. I want to, but I'm needed at the bridge. But I can maybe send Aiden back here to sit with you."

I nod. "Yes. Aiden would be… perfect. Thank you."

Moments later, Aiden steps into my cabin. He's still in his human form, which is both a relief and a disappointment. A relief, because I'm not going to lie. His gray form is downright terrifying to look at. And I'm disappointed because if I'm ever going to get used to it, he's going to need to actually be in that form once in a while.

"You don't have to look like that all the time if you don't want to," I say as he climbs onto the bed. He presses his head back into the pillow and stares up at the ceiling as he gets comfortable. I lie down next to him on my side.

"No? I thought you didn't like my other form. I'm doing this for your benefit."

"I realize that, and it's not that I don't like your other form, it's that I'm not used to it."

He turns to look at me and narrows his eyes. "Sara tells me you weren't afraid of her."

I'm ridden with guilt. Aiden's right, of course. I wasn't afraid of Sara's form. In fact, I thought she looked beautiful.

"I think it's just our pop culture. It's conditioned me to fear you." I reach for his hand and tug it towards my breast. "Please. I want to get to know the real you."

"But this *is* the real me. I'm a shapeshifter, Taryn. All of my forms are me. We might be born a certain way, but that doesn't make any of our chosen forms less real. They're as much a part of me as your eye color."

I open my mouth to reply when the ship starts vibrating somewhere between the first setting on my favorite bullet toy and a washing machine. In other words: it's perfect. It's fun for the first twenty seconds until the dreaded pulling sensation Sara warned me about begins. At first, I swear the room itself is stretching. But like the Haunted Mansion, it's just a trick of my mind.

"It's not really stretching, right?" I ask.

Aiden blinks. "Wh—oh. The room. No, it is. A little, at least. But don't worry, your molecules will go back to their original state in just a few moments. It'll get a little worse before it gets better."

"Fucking… what? *How* is this going to get worse?"

Right on cue, my face begins to melt. Okay, so it doesn't actually melt, but it sure feels like it is. I scream and paw at my face while Aiden cradles me against his chest. He clicks his tongue at me like some sort of mommy hen, trying to soothe me. It works… a little.

"It'll be okay, Taryn. Not much longer now. We're just leaving this galaxy through the wormhole and going to mine."

My head feels two sizes too small, as if my brain is about to dribble out of my ears. My bones buzz inside my body, bringing attention to the fact that I am made out of meat. It's an unsettling, gross feeling, but as promised, it goes away within seconds. The ship stops vibrating, and my stomach gurgles in protest. I can't help but notice Aiden wasn't affected.

"Hey, how come you're okay?" I ask as I look up at him. He reluctantly eases his grip on my waist and lets me roll onto my back. My stomach violently shudders again and for a second, I think I'm going to throw up. I don't. The nausea passes, along with the spinning in front of my eyes.

"I've done this more times than I can count. I got used to it. Human bodies are fragile. But I'm impressed, you didn't vomit!"

I pump my fist into the air and roll my eyes. "Yay, go me..."

Aiden sits up on the bed and reaches forward to curl his fingers around the ends of my hair. I look back at him, and he snatches his hand away, like he's a little boy who just got caught stealing a cookie from the jar.

"It's okay, you can touch me," I say.

He swallows and reaches for my hair again, encouraged. "Sorry, I should have asked first, is all. I like touching you, and it's been over a day. I missed you."

"I've missed you too," I admit. Driving away from the con heartbroken wasn't how I envisioned my weekend ending. It was the one time of the year where I could really cut loose and steep myself in occultism and the paranormal with like-minded people.

"I'm glad to hear that. I was afraid you hated me. Not that I would have blamed you if you did, but... it's nice to know you don't."

I loop my pinky finger around his and smile. "No. I wish you had been more honest up front, but I definitely don't hate you. I don't hate any of you."

"Maybe tell that to Wes," he says as he unhooks his pinky from mine and stands up. "He's barely said a word since we got here."

I bristle. While I don't hate Wes, because hate is an incredibly strong word reserved for the truly foul, I'm not exactly thrilled with him. I watch as Aiden makes his way to the doorway. "He wanted to kidnap me," I say firmly.

Aiden's smile falls, and when he leans against the doorway, his hair falls into his eyes, giving him that sweet, boyish appearance again.

"I know. A decision he made in desperation. He's suffered the worst of the disease back home. Both of his parents succumbed to the sickness, and now his younger sister is ill. I'm not saying this to excuse his actions. I'm merely saying that he acted emotionally."

I draw in a deep breath and nod. While I know forgiveness is a powerful thing, I'm also a firm believer in it being earned. To go from ramming me in my asshole to wanting to kidnap me is an enormous leap.

"I get it. But if he wants my trust back, then he can start by apologizing."

Aiden smiles. "You're right. Wes is… he's difficult, and has a lot to learn. I'm going to go check on the bridge, see how Sara is handling everything. Try to rest, if you can. It's going to be a long journey."

I'm not sure what 'long' even means now that we're in space, but after Aiden leaves, I decide to take his advice. After fluffing the pillows and tossing and turning for god knows how long, I finally drift off into a peaceful sleep.

Chapter Nine

Hours, or maybe it's days later (who knows anymore, I sure don't), I wake to the sound of muffled bickering. I reach for the pillow behind my head and pull it over my face.

"Oh my god, Amber, shut it," I whine into the pillow.

"—push your pride aside for ten seconds. It's important," a male voice says irritably. Wait, who is that? And where am I? My memory fogs over like glass in winter. I'm not in Atlanta anymore, am I? I'm not in Philly, either.

"Guys, stop. I think she's waking up," a woman's voice says. A voice that doesn't belong to Amber. How long have I been asleep? I yank the pillow off of my face and blink open my eyes. I'm not in my hotel room, and I scream.

"Oh, no. Shit, no, honey! It's okay, it's okay!" Sara leaps onto the bed and runs her clawed hand down my head in slow, even strokes. "Shh, you're safe. You're on the ship with me, Aiden, and Wes. Try to remember."

Why does my brain feel so jumbled? I bolt up in the bed and look around. When my eyes lock on Aiden and Wes, I groan and drag my palms down my face.

"... I'm sorry," I mumble. "I forgot where I was."

Wes stands behind Aiden and looks down at his feet sheepishly. The boys are in their human forms, probably erring on the safe side so as not to alarm me when I came to. Sara presses her lips to my temple, sending warmth throughout my entire body. She's so unbelievably kind to me that it's difficult to imagine not having someone like her in my life. I mean, I have Amber, of course. But Amber is my friend. Sara is… Sara makes me yearn for something else beyond platonic friendship and fun hookups.

Oh, shit.

Could I possibly be falling for her?

My face burns from the revelation, but it's short-lived. Once Sara realizes I've calmed down, she gets off the bed and tugs Aiden along with her back to the door. Wes doesn't follow them. He continues to look around the room, anywhere that isn't me.

"Wes, be nice," Aiden warns with a small growl. I don't want them to leave me alone with him, but a conversation with Wes is long overdue, I suppose. After they leave, Wes scratches a spot on his arm and avoids making eye contact.

"Why are you here?" I ask as I cross one leg over the other. I'm not going to hold his hand through this one. If he has something to say to me, then he better say it, otherwise I'm kicking him out.

Finally, he looks up at me, and his eyes flicker with pain.

"I'm sorry," he whispers. I cup my hand around my ear and lean forward, pretending I can't hear him.

"What was that? Sorry, couldn't hear you."

He swallows and drops his arms to his sides. "I said I'm sorry."

I nod as I glare icicles at him. "You're going to have to be a lot more specific, Wes."

He groans like a petulant teenager, and for a second, I swear he's going to stalk out of the room. But to my surprise, he doesn't.

"I was a huge asshole for suggesting we abduct you. It was fucked up of me, and I'm ashamed of how I treated you. I like you a lot, Taryn. It may not seem like it, but I do. I just have a terrible way of showing it," he whispers.

I can't help myself from rolling my eyes. "Okay… well, apology accepted, I guess."

I collapse onto the bed on my back and wait for him to leave. But he doesn't. He clears his throat and steps closer to the bed.

"It doesn't sound like it's accepted. It sounds like the opposite."

I grab a pillow and hug it to my chest. "I'm angry, yes. After sleeping together, I expected better from you, I guess. Aiden told me why you did what you did, but I'm a person, Wes. I don't deserve to be treated that way."

"I agree. I acted out of desperation. I guess Aiden told you my family died, huh?"

I stare up at the ceiling and sigh. That must have been really difficult for him, to watch his parents succumb to a mystery illness they had no cure for. I can't imagine what I'd do if the roles were reversed. What lengths would I truly go to ensure the survival of my loved ones? Would I kidnap someone, take their blood against their will? Maybe, maybe not.

"I'm a person, too. I know I'm a different species from you. I know that. But I'm still a person, and I acted like an asshole because I can't lose my sister. She's the only family I have left, aside from Sara and Aiden."

"I know. Which is why I forgive you. I hope that I can help your sister," I say. Wes gulps in a deep breath like he's about to dive underwater, then releases it. His relief is palpable.

"Really? T-thank you, Taryn. Thank you. You have no idea what it means to hear that."

I sit upright on the bed and lob the pillow, aiming for his head. It smacks him in the face and falls to the ground. Wes stares at me with a bewildered expression.

"What was that for? I don't understand."

I grin. "Just trying to break the tension a little."

He blinks. "O-oh. Okay. Friends, then?"

I shrug. "I guess so. Just promise me one thing?"

"Anything."

Hearing him say that is heartening, but I don't want that kind of promise. I don't want to hold that sort of power over him, either.

"You don't have to do anything. Just promise me you won't try to do anything to me against my will again, okay?"

He nods without hesitation. "Yeah. Of course. I'll always ask."

A moment passes, and then a mischievous idea pops into my head.

"Well, one more thing."

He lifts a brow, then nods. "S-sure?"

"I'd like a kiss, if you wouldn't mind."

Wes's eyes widen at the request, then he walks several paces forward before swooping down to press his lips against mine. The kiss starts off chaste enough until he gently pushes past my lips with his tongue. I moan into his mouth as the heat runs from my face down to the middle of my thighs. Oh, god. He's not just a good kisser. He's excellent. Wes pulls away, giving me time to breathe.

"Was that what you were looking for?" he asks before grinning at me.

I wave my hand in front of my face like a fan. "Whew. Yes, and then some. Although I was wondering if you could ditch the human form?"

He raises his eyebrows as he takes a step back. "What? Why? Don't you like it?"

"I do. But I want to acclimate to your other form. I'm assuming your people don't walk around looking like…" I gesture up and down to my body. "This?"

He laughs. The sound is marvelous. "Not really. I mean, we only chose this form because we were on Earth and wanted to fit in. We maintained it to make you more comfortable. If you're saying you're good with other forms, then so be it." Wes unbuttons his shirt, and I suck in a breath as he lets it drop to the floor. "Are you comfortable in here, by the way? Warm enough? I don't really know how human temperature works. You regulate that on your own, right?"

I nod. "Yeah. Um, it's nice, but…"

The corners of his perfect, statuesque mouth tilt upward. "But it's too bright in here, isn't it?"

"Yeah. Not that I'm ungrateful or anything," I say as I nervously run my fingers through my hair. As if I have a right to whine about a room being too bright when he's been through so much. It feels downright precious of me.

"Aiden didn't give you the rundown of how the room works?" he asks as he tilts his head with a soft grin.

"No? What do you mean by that?"

"I'll show you. Hold on, I'll transform afterwards, if that's okay. This will just take a minute, but it'll be worth it, I promise," he says.

I nod and watch as he walks over to the far-right wall. There's nothing over there, save for white space. It doesn't stop him from running his palm across it, though, and suddenly the room darkens until it's pitch black in here. A chime sounds, and I jump to my feet.

"Hello, Wesliannikos. What can I do for you today?" A woman's voice intones from overhead.

"Hey, Luci. Going to need you to play a scene from Twyla, Sector-561 during Vos," Wes says.

The sentence sounds like gibberish to me, but the voice seems to understand him. Suddenly, the room is awash in a moody, orange glow. Coral pink water kisses a white sandy beach in front of us. Behind me on the bed, brilliant purple trees rustle in the breeze. It all feels so real, so tangible... even the sea breeze smells salty. The fragrance of the trees wafts through my nostrils, enveloping my senses in a scent that's vaguely floral. Like lilacs and citrus combined. It's divine. I can't stop smiling as I spin around, taking in my new surroundings. The sunset low on the horizon, the salty surf filling my lungs–it's almost overwhelming, but I love it.

"How?" I ask. It's the only thing I can think to say.

He laughs and holds his hand out for me to take. "It's one of my favorite spots back home. Sorry for the spoilers, but I figured it'd be better than a white room."

"It's perfect," I say, and take his hand. He pulls me against his naked chest and holds me in a gentle embrace. I close my eyes and let the sounds of the waves lull me into a calm, meditative-like state until his voice interrupts my reverie.

"I'm glad you think so. I'm also glad your species enjoys hugs as much as we do."

I chuckle against his warm, bare skin. "Some things are just universal, I guess."

Chapter Ten

Sitting on another planet's beach with a real, live alien wasn't on my Chimera Con bingo card, but I'm happy with the way things are going so far. Wes, now in his gray alien form, holds me close as we watch the pink waves crash against the shore.

"What do you think of my home, Taryn?" he asks. His voice is a gentle hum in my mind. It's hard to think I was ever terrified of him and Aiden. Acclimation time really was all I needed, I guess.

"It's gorgeous. Thank you for getting me out of the cabin for a little while," I say.

Wes can't smile, not really. But I can tell how he's feeling from the way his emotions tickle at the back of my mind, like a gentle caress. He's happy.

"I'm glad you think so. Technically, we haven't gone anywhere, but…"

I shrug. "Yeah, I know. Still, it's nice to be somewhere without walls."

"I can't wait to show you all of this in person," he murmurs.

Minutes pass, and while I'm content to sit in silence as we listen to the waves, there are a few questions nagging me, begging to be answered.

"So… you, Aiden, and Sara, huh?" I look up at him with a lopsided grin.

He stares straight ahead, unblinking. "Yes. On Earth, I guess you'd call them my partners. Or boyfriend and girlfriend. We've been together for a while, though time works a little differently out here. It's hard to quantify. Let's just say we've yearned for one another for a very long time." He presses his forehead against mine, and my heart does a little somersault in my breast. "And we could love you, too."

I draw in a deep breath as my insides twist into knots.

"You don't seem to be very happy with that thought," he says in a quiet voice.

I shake my head and lean against his shoulder. "It's not that. It's just…"

It's just that I was literally dumped by my boyfriend of five years only days ago. Now I have a triad of aliens asking me to join them. It's not that I can't see myself with the three of them. But it doesn't seem like the rational thing to do, no matter what my heart is telling me.

"Wes, I love the idea of joining you three. I really do. But Brandon just dumped me. We were together for a while. Lived together. Planned on getting married."

His enormous eyes blink slowly as he watches me, like he's waiting for the drop of the guillotine that would sever our already fragile connection.

"Yeah. I get that. According to Aiden, the guy was a real asshole unworthy of you," he says. The bitterness in his voice is obvious.

"And that's probably true, but going immediately from one monogamous relationship to a polyamorous one with three aliens is… it's a bit much. For now, at least."

He dips his head forward as his eyes turn glassy. Oh, no. I've hurt him. Dammit, this was the last thing I wanted to do to Wes. I wrap my arm around his shoulder. His skin in this form is cool to the touch, a sharp contrast from how he normally feels in his human flesh.

"I care about you three and would love to see where this goes, but I think we need to slow down."

Wes's tongue flicks between his lips like a snake's. For once, I can't tell what he's thinking or how he's feeling because he's putting up walls. Psychic walls? Is that a thing? Before I can speak, we're interrupted by the sound of another chime from overhead.

"Sara and Aiden are requesting permission to enter the cabin," the woman's voice intones. "What are your commands, Wesliannikos?"

Wes looks up at the starry sky and growls.

"Let them in," he mutters, obviously displeased by the interruption.

A doorway opens in the middle of the beach like a portal, and Sara steps over the threshold onto the sand wearing a loose-fitting white linen dress. Aiden enters behind her, only this time he's not in his human form. When Sara spots me cuddled up next to Wes, her eyes flicker with amusement.

"See? I told you, Aiden," she practically purrs. Aiden blinks slowly as he looks us up and down.

"No, cuddling doesn't count. You said they'd be fucking."

Sara scowls at Aiden. She's so much taller than he is in this form, so elegant and lovely to behold. Her alabaster skin shimmers against the light of the distant planets, giving her an ethereal glow. Aiden, on the other hand, nearly blends in with the darkness so well I have to squint to see him as he steps closer. Wes makes a few odd clicking noises inside his mouth as Aiden approaches.

"We took bets on whether you'd be fighting or fucking. I said fighting, Sara predicted fucking," Aiden explains telepathically.

I do my best to smile, but it's difficult. Wes and I were on the verge of an argument, I think, and their timing couldn't have been worse. Not only that, but I don't appreciate them taking bets on what he and I were getting up to in private. I push myself up to stand beside Wes and cross my arms over my chest.

"That's a bit rude, isn't it? Well, as you can see, it's neither. So I guess neither of you wins," I say bitterly.

Sara and Aiden look at one another and wince.

"I apologize," Aiden says, looking back at me. "We didn't mean anything by it. Just trying to keep things lighthearted, but I understand how inappropriate that was. We are happy you two are getting along, though." Aiden's gaze drifts down to Wes, who continues to stare at the ocean, unblinking. "Wes? Are you okay?"

"I'm fine," he mutters.

"Wes. Remember what we talked about? C'mon, man. Up. Up, up, up!" Aiden nudges Wes with his foot until finally, Wes leaps to his feet with a grumble. "Don't get snippy with me, Wesli. Let's go to the bridge, talk it out. Anyankos said we need to communicate better."

Anyankos? Who is that? I haven't heard them mention that name before.

Wes turns and narrows his dark eyes into thin slits, but Aiden isn't deterred by his grumpiness. He laces his claws with Wes's and leads him along the sand, back through the doorway. Sara and I watch them go until the door shuts behind them.

I have no idea what just happened, but I know I'm responsible for Wes's change in mood. He and I had been doing so well, but then I had to go and ruin it. Why do I always ruin everything? Sara turns to look at me tenderly, then holds up her phone.

"Want to see what I found earlier?" she chirps, as though the earlier drama had never happened.

I nod. "Um, sure? But, are those two going to be okay? I didn't mean to put Wes in such a bad mood."

Sara rolls her beautiful, blue eyes before sitting down in the sand. She pats the spot beside her and waits for me. When I join her, she huddles up against me and holds up her phone so I can see the screen.

"Don't worry about them. Anyankos is a community elder back home, kind of like a relationship therapist. They've been seeing her for a while, and she gave them a few tools to use when things get rocky. They'll be just fine."

A therapist? That makes sense, now. I had asked Brandon if he'd be willing to do couples therapy a couple years ago, but he shot me down.

"I wish I had your confidence. He told me he…" I hesitate. This probably isn't something I should be telling her, but it's something that directly involves her. "… He said that you, as in the three of you, could love me too. And I told him that while it was a tempting offer, I was just dumped by my boyfriend and needed time. I think that's why he's upset."

Sara's eyes flicker from blue to gold, then back to blue. She emits a small groan before saying, "Oh, Wes. His heart is… far too big for his body, I'm afraid."

My own heart sinks into my stomach.

"That's not to say we wouldn't love to keep you. We would," she continues. "But we understand your situation all too well. It's a miracle to us that you even chose to come along willingly! We've been searching for a willing donor for ages now."

I snicker and look up at the canopy of stars that twinkle above us. God, it's mesmerizing. It's difficult to believe that in every single one of those twinkling dots is an entire galaxy full of planets, and quite possibly, other life forms. Sara follows my gaze and lets out a soft, whistle-like sound.

"Once upon a time, I was from one of those stars, just like you."

I look back at her, and notice her eyes have turned dark purple. I'm not sure what the color-changing irises mean, but if I were to guess, it had something to do with her emotions.

"What happened? You're not from Wes's and Aiden's planet, then?"

She shakes her head. "I am not. I'm from a lovely planet once known as Euphorra. It was a verdant, lush place. Full of rainforests, powerful oceans, mountains that kissed the heavens."

I frown. The way she speaks of her home world makes me nervous. This story isn't going to have a happy ending.

"But the planet died due to an invasive species that was let loose when a neighboring species paid us a visit. They didn't know. It wasn't on purpose, but… once it was loose, it proliferated at an alarming rate. Our home was destroyed within weeks, and when our people petitioned for aid, it was Aiden's planet that answered. Unfortunately, there was nothing left to save. My people were too slow to act. Most of our people starved to death, and those who survived became refugees," she says before sucking down a breath. She's fighting off tears. I wrap an arm around her shoulder and give her a gentle squeeze, and she smiles at me.

"Thank you for listening. I figured… we know about your home, and so much about your people. But you don't know anything about mine, or theirs. It's not fair."

I catch a tear that trickles down her cheek and wipe it away.

"Mm, a lot of things in life unfortunately aren't very fair. That's terrible.

I'm so sorry, god. I couldn't imagine what it would be like to lose my home like that."

She rests her head against my shoulder as we listen to the gentle caress of the waves on the shore. "I hope you never have to experience such a thing."

We sit like this, tangled up in one another's arms for a long while until she lets out a long yawn. Her lithe body is wrapped up like a very cute pretzel, but when she catches me watching, she sits upright. "Oh, I nearly forgot. I was so busy talking I didn't get to show you what I found on my phone!"

Oh, right. I had forgotten all about that. Sara unlocks the screen and pulls up a familiar looking sight: the front page of NewTube, the video hosting site I use to upload my vlogs. And… I gape in horror when I see exactly what channel she's navigated to.

"Sara, is that—"

"Yes!" Sara squeals in delight as she presses play on the little video, and a girl around twenty-five years old starts blabbering about demons versus ghosts. The girl's complexion is sheet-white, with dark rimmed charcoal eyes and pin straight jet-black hair. She's also wearing a black hoodie dress three sizes too big for her small frame. I let out a long, agonizing groan because the girl I'm seeing on the screen? She's me.

Sara looks at me, clearly confused by my reaction.

"What? What's wrong? You look so adorable in this video! I've gone through at least fifty of your videos so far. It's so interesting to see how much you've evolved in such a short span of time…"

"Sara, please." I cover my face with my hands, trying to hide. But there is no hiding from Sara, not when she has you in her crosshairs.

"Please what? You really are a cute little bean, aren't you? Humans are the cutest species I've come across so far. Your hair, the way you cover your bodies in clothing, your sexual rituals. I love all of it. I've been emulating your fashion. It's a lot of fun!"

Holy shit, Sara might actually be like a… oh crap, what does Amber call the people who are really, really into Japanese culture? Weebs? Sara might actually be a weeb, but for humanity.

"So, is that why you're working so hard with Wes and Aiden? Because of your own planet?" I ask, trying to deflect from the embarrassment on the screen. Ugh. Hearing my own voice makes me want to walk into the ocean and never return.

"What?" Sara tears her attention from the screen—thank goodness—and gapes at me like an innocent fawn caught in headlights. "Oh. You mean scouting other planets for a cure. Yes. I signed up years ago in order to give back to the people who saved my life. It's the least I can do, you know?"

Years. They've been dealing with this mystery illness for years. I can't even imagine how horrific that must be for them.

I nod. "It's definitely admirable. And what about Wes and Aiden, then?"

"They were already a mated pair when I met them. The three of us were thrown together as a team, and… one thing led to another, and here we are." Sara looks back at her phone and giggles. "Is this what you do, then? As your job? You make instructional videos about ghosts?"

I pry the phone away from her claws and pause the video so I don't have to hear my younger self's voice any longer. "I used to, but I focus primarily on cryptids and UFOs now. Or did. I don't think I'll be uploading anything else once I get back, though."

Sara licks her bottom lip. "Why? These are great! You have a wonderful personality on the screen and adorable, too. It's no wonder you have so many subscribers."

I shrug. "Yeah, but now that I know everything I'm talking about is a load of shit, I don't think I can do it anymore."

Wait. How the hell are we even getting 4G out here? Full bars! How is that possible?

"Sara, how is it we're able to access the internet out here?"

Sara snickers as she takes her phone back from me. "I could explain it to you, but it would take a while. Is it okay if I just say it's advanced tech stuff?"

In other words, it's space magic I'll never comprehend. All of this makes me realize just how primitive of a species humanity truly is. I can't even get full bars inside my apartment. I dig out my own phone and look at the screen out of curiosity. The screen still says it's Tuesday, September 6th. I have one missed text from Amber asking me if I made it to D.C. yet.

"You haven't missed much time back home. Now that, I couldn't explain to you even if I tried, because I failed wormhole science back at the academy. Wes is the egghead around here, though. You could ask him, though he'd probably rant about your Ethan Graywick again."

I don't even bother to correct her as I blink back my surprise. "I'm sorry, what? Wormhole? We went through a wormhole, and I somehow missed it?"

She nods. "Yes. Is that so strange?" Sara leans in, kisses me on the cheek, and scoops my hands into her lap to trace her claws against my palms. My poor brain. My poor, squishy human brain. It's liable to explode soon, so I'm just going to go back to my mantra from earlier: don't overthink it. Overthinking is the enemy.

She doesn't say anything else for a while, which is good because I don't really feel like talking anymore. Now that I've been on a real, live alien ship, it's not as though I can start making videos speculating about them. My new friends don't have to threaten me, or even ask me not to talk about my experiences out here. I'm smart enough to know that the government is likely going to have a little 'chat' with me the second I step onto Earth soil, if the testimonies of abductees can be believed. The men in black? White vans pulling up in front of houses? I'm expecting the full nine yards when I get home and I'll be disappointed if I don't get it.

I run my fingers through my hair and cringe when I realize I haven't had a shower in… well, I'm not sure how long and it doesn't really matter, because I stink.

"I feel gross," I say.

Sara pulls me to my feet and twirls me once like we're in the middle of a dance. "Then we need to get you into the shower, sweetheart."

I don't know why I assumed the aliens didn't have a shower on their ship, but it makes sense. None of them smell off-putting, so they probably enjoy proper hygiene just as much as I do.

"Luci, reset cabin parameters to default please," she says as she looks up at the sky.

"Command accepted, Sarannia. One moment please," the feminine voice says from overhead.

The room immediately fades to black, and when the lights come back on, the cabin is back to the way it was before Wes turned it into a paradise. No more ocean breeze, no more wind in my hair, and no more waves rolling against the shore. Sara notices the disappointment etched on my face and smiles sympathetically.

"Maybe once we're done cleaning you up, I can take you on a tour of my home planet. It's been a while since I visited, even in a dream," she says, and I notice the sadness that colors her every syllable. It must be difficult for her, not having a home to go back to. Not wanting to dwell on sadness, Sara leads me down a plain white hallway that goes on forever until we reach a three-way fork in the path.

"Showers on the left, straight ahead is the bridge, and to the right are the other cabins. We don't really use them, though. We sleep together in a single cabin," she says before leading me down the hallway where the showers are located. "The shower is like the cabin. You can ask Luci to change the scenery to anything you'd like so long as it exists in reality."

I nod as I follow her. Her long, white dress flutters behind in a gossamer train. It reminds me of a moth's wing. "And what if... I wanted company in this shower?"

Sara stops abruptly, pivots on her heel, and grins. "Who would you like to join you? One of the boys, or may I recommend myself?"

"You may. In fact, I was hoping you would," I say as I hold out my hand for her to take.

"Then I'm honored. Come on, let me show you how it works."

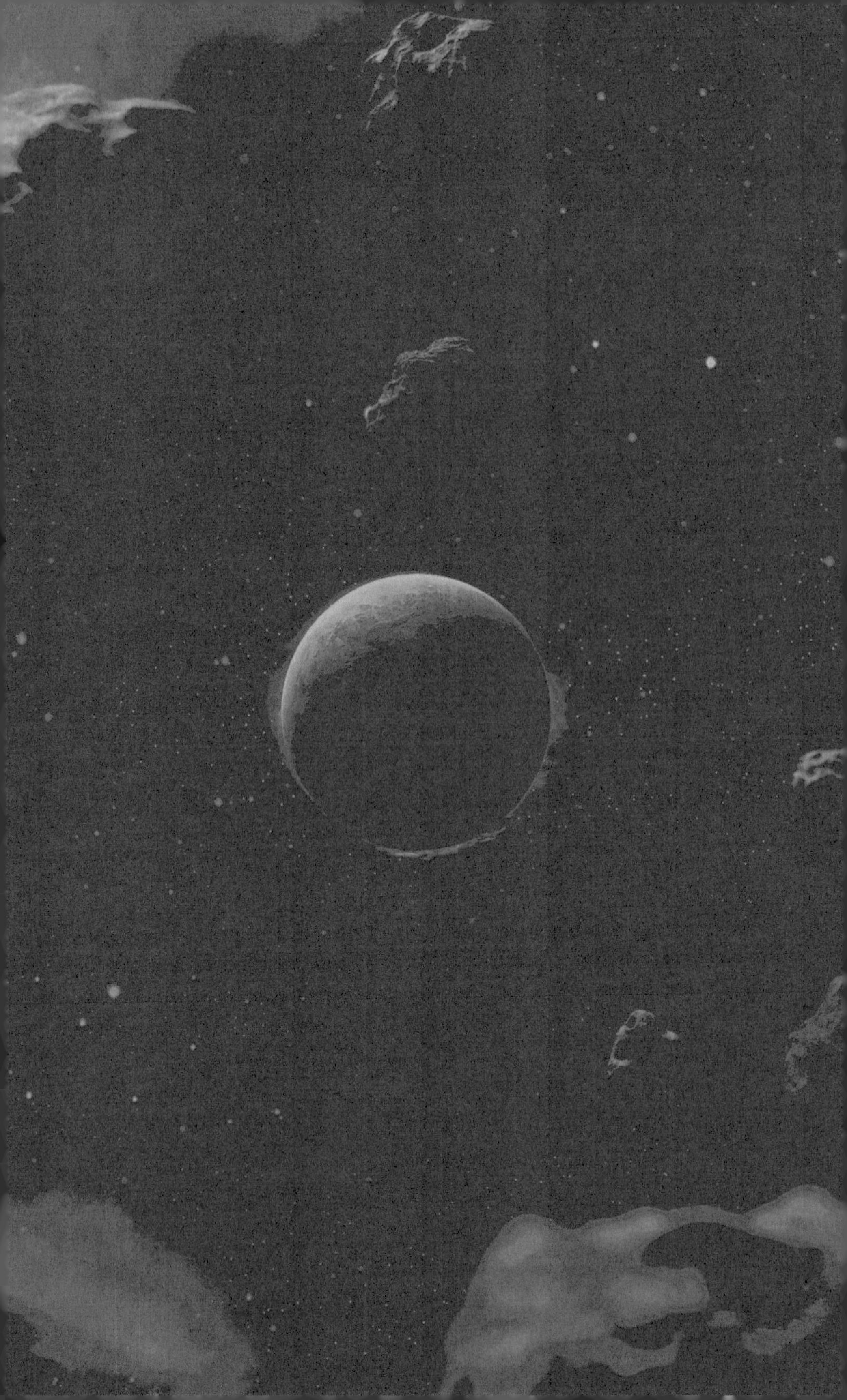

Chapter Eleven

Sara wasn't kidding when she said the showers could be turned into anything, and she wastes no time in showing me how to activate Luci to input commands. The shower itself is like the rest of the ship. Clean to the point of being sterile and so bright, it hurts my eyes. The showerhead hangs from the center of the room, with a drain in the middle of the floor. It's just… a big, empty, white room.

"So, it's important when asking Luci for a change of scenery to be as specific as you can. Luci, change shower room one to Euphorra, starglow season, please."

I tilt my head and watch as the room is plunged into total darkness. At first, I worry that I won't be able to see anything. And then the glow part of Starglow starts to happen. Plant life rustles all around us, and leaves come to life with the bright, cerulean glow of bioluminescence. I gasp as I struggle to take it all in.

"Isn't it beautiful?" she says. "Let's get you out of your clothes."

Sara is slow and methodical at first, taking her time to unzip my dress in the back until it stops just above the corset. I appreciate the care she gives to my clothing. After all, this dress cost a small fortune and I'm protective of it.

She presses her lips to the crook of my neck as she slides the caps of my dress down my shoulders. I shudder from the sudden contact, and she pulls away.

"Is this okay? I can stop if you'd rather get undressed yourself. I know things have been stressful," she says.

I shake my head and meet her gaze. "No, this is perfect, thank you. Kiss me again."

And she does. She kisses me again and again along my neck, dotting a little trail down my collarbone until she reaches the top of my breast. Her eyes drink me in as she waits for my signal. Goosebumps rise on my skin along with the hair on the back of my neck, and a familiar heat emanates between my thighs. I want her. I want her a little too much, and I can't keep myself from begging.

"Please," I whimper. "Please touch me as much as you want."

Her lips curl into a small smile as she twirls me around again, this time to unlace my corset. "This looks like it was difficult to put on," she murmurs as she slips her claws through the black ribbons of silk. "Don't worry, I'll make sure not to hurt it." She's patient as she unlaces the corset, then sets it aside in the grass where it won't be disturbed.

Everything about Sara—or I guess Sarannia--is graceful, and it's with grace she treats every inch of my body. I inhale the scent of damp soil, fragrant flowers I don't recognize, and petrichor as she shimmies my skirt down over my hips. She slips a claw underneath the lace trim of my pastel blue thong and purrs as she examines it.

"I like this lacey little thing you're wearing," she murmurs in my ear. Every cell in my body is on fire. I need her to touch me, and I need her *now*. Sensing my impatience, she kisses the area between my shoulder blades and pulls my near-naked form against her breasts. "Relax, sweet thing. We have all the time in the universe to explore one another. Why rush it?"

She's right. There's no sense in rushing something that's meant to be savored. Her arms come around my middle to embrace me, and for a moment, I'm worried she's going to put her claws in places I'm not sure I want them. Delicate places.

"Sara, um... your claws," I mutter as she kisses the top of my head.

"What about them, sweet thing?"

The only other sound in the room is the chirping of nocturnal bugs and occasional howl of a... wolf? No, probably not, seeing as this isn't Earth. I swallow as I turn around to look her up and down.

"I won't hurt you, if that's what's concerning you. I have other methods for delivering pleasure that don't involve pain." Her eyes glow in a shade of vibrant gold as she strokes my cheek with her claw. "Unless you're into that sort of thing like I am?"

I pause. I've never been a very adventurous person in bed. Never experimented with kink before, and never tried out more interesting positions. It's not that I didn't want to. But things with Brandon were just... comfortable. Or lazy. It's hard to tell the difference sometimes.

"I don't know," I whisper. It's the only answer I can give her right now. She nods, then slithers out of her slinky dress, allowing it to pool at her feet on the floor. I thought she was beautiful before with her clothes on, but now that she's naked before me? Oh, fuck. Her pristine scales shimmer in the moonlight and pulse with the same blue glow from the plants that surround us. While her face is full of sharp angles, her body moves like a watercolor painting. Smooth, rounded strokes that make her appear soft, suggesting the duality of her true nature.

Her breasts are just as perfect in this form as they were in her human disguise. Perky, round mounds that rest high on her chest, but when I get a closer look, I notice there are no nipples in the center. She also doesn't have a navel, but that's not a surprise. She pushes the dress aside with her foot and looks up at the ceiling. "Luci, set shower one to Euphorra mist, please."

Within seconds, the room fills with warm steam. "We can experiment, if you'd like."

I nod slowly and lick my bottom lip. "Y-yes, I would like that. Do I need a safe word?"

She chuckles and lifts a hand to her mouth. "No, darling. The safe word is 'stop.' If you don't like something, say so. Does that sound good?"

"Perfect," I murmur. Sara cranes her neck forward and kisses me deeply for several seconds before dragging one of her claws against the back of my neck. The mist in the room envelops us like a thick, warm embrace. It's not exactly what I had in mind when I came in here to shower, but it's definitely better.

Beneath my feet is spongy soil soft enough to sit on, and Sara lowers me down into the damp leaves. I've never fucked outside before. Does this even count if we're technically still inside the ship?

"What's on your mind?" she asks as she cradles my body against hers. "I can see the wheels turning in your head. It's cute, but if something's bothering you, please tell me."

I bite my lip. "When you mentioned pain before, what did you mean by that?"

I can't deny that I'm a little curious. I'm not naïve, I know what BDSM is, in theory. But it's not like I've actually witnessed it being practiced, and I haven't brushed up on the concept through porn or books. Sara leans in to nip the tender flesh of my skin, and I shiver.

"We can start off simple. On my home world, my people enjoyed the concept of owning others as pets," she says casually, as if making normal conversation.

I bristle and pull away. "Pets? You can't own people, Sara. That's wrong."

To her credit, she smiles at me with tenderness. "No, sweetheart. Not like that. Everything is consensual. It's a game we'd play with our partners. In this case, you would be my little pet and bow to my every command."

Her little pet. I swallow hard as I consider her proposition.

"What does a pet have to do, exactly?" I ask.

She presses her nose against mine and nuzzles it. "A pet submits to their owner, within reason, of course. We talk about boundaries first. Things you want to do, things you may wish to do but are unsure, and things you won't do."

I nod. "With you so far. Well, I tried anal for the first time with Wes and liked that."

"Yes. You were very brave with that, pet." She cups my face between her palms. "Even I won't do that with him. I don't care for it. Is there anything you definitely don't like?"

I nibble my bottom lip as I consider her question. "Well, sometimes Brandon would try dirty talk in the bedroom, but he'd end up calling me things. Rude things. I didn't like that."

She furrows her brow in deep thought. "Really? No, I would never call you anything cruel, pet. Is there anything else?"

I shake my head. "I don't think so."

"This will be fun, then. We will find out what you like… together."

Sara never loses the tenderness in her voice as she speaks to me. "We won't do anything you don't like, pet. Even though you're my pet for now, you are still in control of your experience. How about I show you a few of my favorite toys?"

I may not be sure what sorts of kink I'm into, but toys sound a lot more my speed. I'm no stranger to vibrators, though it's not as though I've used them very often lately. There were nights when Brandon wouldn't be able to get me there, and that's when the bullet under my pillow would come in handy.

Sara looks up at the ceiling and blinks her round, golden eyes. "Luci. Send electro-clamps to shower one, please."

"Affirmative, Sarannia. Electro-clamps materializing. Please stand by," Luci's voice chimes. I flinch as a pair of small metal instruments appear in Sara's hands, as if by magic. The silver gadgets look like they belong in a car maintenance shop and are linked together with a delicate silver chain. They're beautiful, but I have no idea what they're used for. I'm a little skittish that Sara called them 'electro clamps', though.

"How do we use those?" I ask, almost too afraid to hear the answer. Sara pinches the clamps, showing me how they work. My eyes widen as they open and close.

"Do those go where I think they go?"

She nods. "Oh, yes. Yes, they most certainly do, pet. But don't worry about these for right now." Sara sets the clamps down in a patch of grass beside my thighs. "Right now, I would like to explore your body. Learn what gets your blood pumping. What makes you squirm." She trails her claws along my bare stomach and past my navel until she reaches my inner thigh.

I breathe in shallow, quick breaths as she scrapes her claws along the outside of my labia.

"Yes," I whisper. "That sounds good."

"Luci. General probe to shower one, please," Sara says. Another small metal instrument materializes in Sara's hand bit by bit, only this one doesn't look as intimidating. It's a small metal tube, not unlike my bullet back home. "Oh, and lube, too."

"Right. Can't forget that," I say with a chuckle. Sara smiles gently as a bottle of lubricant takes shape beside her ankle. The small, metal bottle looks plain enough that no one would give it a second thought. Silly me for thinking there would be some sort of weird alien space lube out here. She pumps a pea-size amount of pink gel onto her fingertips and rubs her hands together, warming it.

I lick my bottom lip in anticipation as she readies the lubricant, but instead of going for my cunt like I expect her to, she massages the gel over my breasts. The heat that radiates from her palms is instantaneous and stars burst in front of my eyes. As she massages the gel in slow, sensual movements, my nipples start to tingle.

"Oh," I mutter. It feels like cinnamon oil being rubbed on my nipples, but it's not unpleasant. In fact, I think I love it.

Sara snickers at my reaction and flicks her tongue around my nipple. The coolness of her tongue mixed with the warmth of the lubricant is an exciting combination. I tilt my head back and moan from the new, welcome sensation.

"Good? I love this stuff," she murmurs before licking my other nipple in a circle. I press my back up against a soft, grassy knoll, placing myself at a more comfortable angle. Sara takes the silver probe and runs it against the outside of my labia. It's cool, and I gasp from the sudden switch in temperature. "Let me know if anything is too overwhelming," she says.

Sara continues to suck on my nipples with vigor, and I watch as they pucker into rigid peaks in her mouth. Her tongue feels incredible, so incredible I can't keep my pelvis down in the grass. I raise my hips up, and she presses me back down into the grass with the heel of her palm. She sucks my nipple hard, then pops it out of her mouth, leaving a tendril of saliva clinging to her bottom lip. Sara wipes her mouth clean and snickers.

"Slow, sweet thing. I will get to your delicious cunt soon, but we don't want to rush this moment, do we?"

I moan in frustration. Maybe forcing me to be patient is her idea of pain? It certainly seems so.

"Fine," I say with a huff. Sara raises an eyebrow and wags a finger in my eyes.

"Ah, ah, pet. Let's disperse with that naughty attitude of yours."

"Yes, mistress," I say sarcastically. Sara's eyes flash a bright amber, and for a second, I'm afraid she's angry with me.

"Mistress? You cheeky little thing. Now I'm going to insist you call me that from now on," she purrs.

I groan with mock irritation, but I honestly love it. I love being her pet, love having her take care of me, love being her little experiment.

Sara licked, sucked, pinched, and flicked my nipples until I was slicker than ice. My cunt pulses with desperate need, and if it didn't get fed soon, there was no telling how much longer I could survive. I let loose a growl, and Sara finally releases my nipples from their torment to…

… Turn to the nipple clamps in the grass.

My breath catches as I watch her ready them.

"You're sadistic," I say playfully as she picks the clamps up and pinches them in front of me.

"Ah, no. It's you're 'sadistic, *mistress*.' Say it slowly now, and this time, without the bratty tone," she narrows her eyes at me, and I nod slowly.

"You're sadistic, mistress," I repeat evenly.

She laughs, satisfied with my obedience, and presses one of the cool clamps against my nipple, which is so hard it could cut stone.

"Yes?" Sara asks, her eyes wide and curious.

"Yes," I say.

"Good, thank you." Sara presses her lips against mine in a sweet kiss before setting the clamp on one of my nipples. I hiss at the sudden pinch. It's a lot harder than Sara's fingers, but once I acclimate to the pain, it's not so bad.

"How does that feel?" she asks.

I nod. "It's fine so far."

She places the clamp on my other nipple, then takes both of my breasts in her hands to squeeze them together as she admires her handiwork. "Perfect. You have the best tits for this, pet."

I smirk. "Oh? Are there wrong tits for this?"

She rolls her eyes and runs her claws along the swell of my breasts, making me shiver.

"Sassy little thing," she says with a wink, then moves down between my legs to spread my thighs open as far as they will go. The mist in the room is still going strong, creating a beautiful, glossy appearance on Sara's skin. Droplets of water hang on my eyelashes and I can barely see save for what's right in front of my face. For all I know, this is all part of Sara's plan: Blind me so I can't see what's coming, relish in my surprised gasps and whimpers. It was diabolical.

"I'm going to make you scream until you're hoarse, pet," she coos before dragging her tongue between my folds, taking her sweet time to taste and savor me. She groans along with me as she flicks her tongue in and out of my cunt. Then she finds the hood of my clit and runs the tip of her tongue around it in languid circles. My hips buck, and she presses her hand down onto my stomach to hold me down. She raises her head to glare up at me from between my thighs.

"Ass in the dirt, pet," she says, more firmly this time. "I won't tell you again."

Her commands are soft but firm, with just the right amount of edge in her voice to make me want to listen to her. She lowers her head back down and sucks on my clit with more enthusiasm. Oh, god. If she keeps this up, it won't be long before I come. I thrust my fingernails into the dirt at my sides and grab onto the tufts of grass like they're a head full of hair. I moan, and she moans along with me until I can't take it anymore. Sara devours my pussy until I'm grinding against her face. To my surprise, she doesn't stop me. I'm on the precipice of a strong orgasm when suddenly she yanks her face away, and I let out a low growl of agony.

"No! I was almost there!"

Sara tosses her head back and laughs. She really is sadistic, fuck.

"Now, now, pet. The more we delay your climax, the better it'll be, I promise." She smirks cruelly at me. My own gaze is intense and heady, and I want to scream and cry but I know that won't get me what I desperately crave. "Besides, I still have to probe you."

Sara leans down to grab the bottle and squirts some gel into her hands. She rubs the lubricant between her palms slowly as my thighs quake. The blood gathered in my clit begins to flow in the other direction, the threat of my orgasm fading away.

"Are you okay, pet?" Sara asks in a low, dark voice. I bristle and yank at the grass at my sides.

"Yes, mistress," I say through gritted teeth.

Then she leans forward and applies the lubricant to my cunt in slow, even movements. My hips jerk up, and predictably, she places the heel of her palm on top of my pelvis to guide my ass down. She's grinning, but I know she has something up her sleeve.

"Naughty, pet. What did I say about rushing me? Just for that, I'm going to delay your orgasm even longer now," she says with a wink.

"Wait, what?!" I gasp, but before I can react, she places the probe inside of me. The cold metal within my pussy leaves me feeling so full it's enough to distract me from the ache in my nipples. I bite my bottom lip as she swivels the probe around in circular movements.

"How does this feel?" she asks as she moves the probe around inside me.

"It's fine," I say. "But a little boring compared to your tongue. My toys back home at least have the decency to vibrate."

And then the probe starts to pulse in strong, rapid movements. Sara releases the probe and watches with glee as the little bullet burrows into my slit without her guidance.

"What the—"

"Shh, relax my pet," she whispers. I suck in a deep breath as the probe pulses deep within me and radiates a gentle heat. It feels sublime, and I toss my head back as I shudder. My entire body quakes with pleasure, and I feel my climax surging once again. Sara sits primly beside me, clearly happy with her work. With the nipple clamps on my tits and the probe inside my cunt doing all the work for her, what else is there for her to do besides watch?

"Ah, this is a lovely view," she says in a sing-songy voice. "Thank you for letting me play with you, pet."

I let loose another scream and hope it doesn't disturb Aiden and Wes. Sara laughs and holds out her hand at the entrance of my cunt. The little probe slides out of me and into her hand. I moan in disappointment.

"Oh, don't be that way. I told you I wasn't letting you come that easy," she says.

"Sara, please," I beg. I'm not proud of the fact that I'm begging, but I need to come, and I need to come *now*. "Please."

Sara purses her lips, as though considering my pleas, then repositions herself on top of me in a straddle. Still holding the probe in her hand, she presses a silver knob onto its end, then pulls on it to lengthen it like a cane. I marvel at its elegant, rounded tips and silently wish it was still inside of me. As though reading my thoughts, Sara carefully places one end of the probe into my cleft. I whimper in ecstasy as the probe warms my cunt again, but she doesn't stop there; she wriggles her hips against my pelvis and twists the probe, pointing it upward. I watch in both arousal and fascination as she gently guides the bent end into herself.

Oh, things are getting interesting now.

A *lot* more interesting.

The probe pulses and radiates its sensual heat through my cunt, and I arch my back. I grab my breasts and moan. I almost forgot the nipple clamps were still there, too distracted by other more… pressing… matters.

Sara begins to moan along with me until our cries of pleasure fill the entire room. Luckily, the sounds of the night creatures around us drown out our screams as we fuck the probe vigorously together. Sharing a toy with the woman I'm enamored with has to be the hottest thing I've ever experienced in my life, and if my body would let me, I'd keep this up all night long.

"Fuck!" she screams as she grabs my breasts and presses them together.

"I'm going to come soon, pet, but not before you. Are you close?"

Oh, if only she knew. I've been dying to get off the second she touched me.

"Y-yes," I pant. I buck my hips against the probe and watch as it slides in and out of her slick, wet cunt. She gropes my breasts, taking care not to agitate the clamps too much.

"Tell me when you're coming, you have my permission," she growls.

I stare up at the sky, which I know in the back of my mind is still just the ceiling. But right now? All I see is a galaxy of stars shining brightly above me. For the second time since meeting the trio, I'm going to see stars when I come.

Beads of sweat drip down my neck and across the curve of my breasts, mixing with the rivulets of water from the mist. I grind my hips, urging the probe inside of my cunt deeper and deeper until something inside of me snaps. My eyes widen, and I let out a cry from deep within my belly.

"Oh, fuck! Sara, I'm coming! I'm coming!"

I buck against the probe and her body as the sounds of wet slapping joins the chorus of our moans. As the orgasm washes over me, wave after wave, she removes the clamps carefully but quickly. "Yes!" I shriek.

Sara's own orgasm comes on just as strong, and her cries of pleasure only add to my own.

We lay there in the middle of the shower-turned-alien-rainforest and collapse into each other's arms. Together we stay like that for at least thirty minutes before Luci chimes in to check on us.

"Do either of you require medical aid?" Luci asks in a flat voice.

"No, no, Luci. We're just fine. Thank you," Sara says as she waves her hand above her head flippantly. She presses her lips to my forehead and snickers. "Sorry, sweetie. We should probably get you into a proper bed, though."

"Yeah, that's not a bad idea in theory, but. Um. I can't really use my legs," I say.

Sara sighs and pushes herself up to stand. "Okay, then it looks like I'm carrying you."

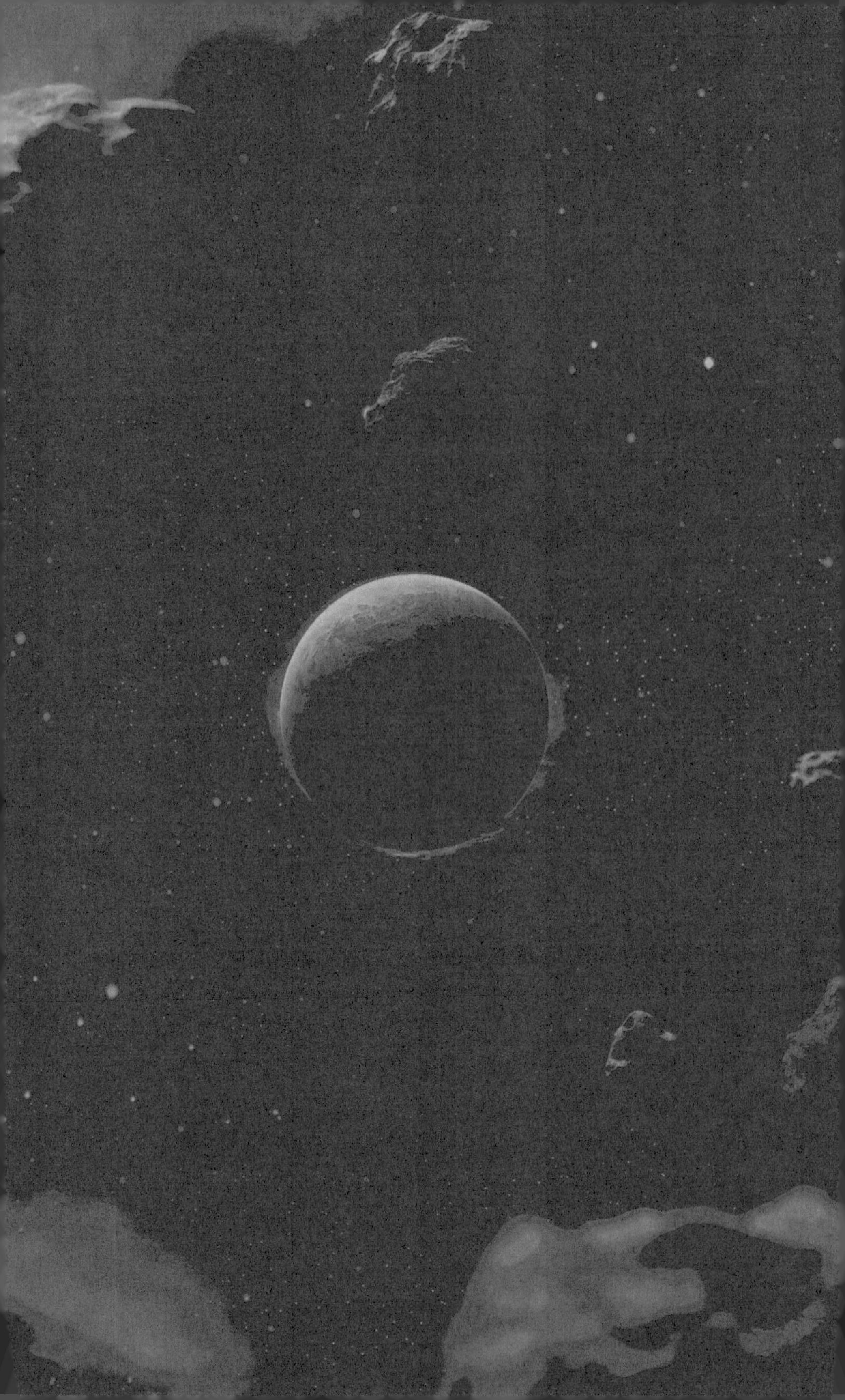

Chapter Twelve

Sara carries me to bed and tucks me underneath the blankets and sheets before kissing me chastely on my forehead. She crawls underneath the blankets and snuggles beside me, her long, sinewy frame curling around me like a protective barrier against the outside world.

"I know what we did wasn't too strenuous, but I'm staying with you tonight to be sure you don't drop," she murmurs into my ear. I wriggle my backside against her body, relishing in being the little spoon.

"Drop? What do you mean?" I ask.

Sara presses her lips to my shoulders, and I shiver against her touch.

"In your language, I suppose it would be called a sub drop. After a scene, you are much more likely to have an endorphins crash. It's unpleasant, and I don't want that to happen to you. So, we'll take as long as we need to, in order to make sure you're feeling loved and comfortable. I also have a pill to give you."

I twist around to look at her with a wide-eyed expression.

"Don't worry. The pill is perfectly safe for human consumption. It's been tested extensively. My people use it all the time back home, and we've used it on humans before."

Do I even want to know? But knowing Sara and the others, whatever was done to the other humans was most likely met with enthusiastic consent.

"Okay," I murmur. We spend the next hour cuddling, kissing, and exploring each other's bodies with gentle touches. The scales that cover her thighs and collarbone are fascinating to me, and she lets me take as much time as I like marveling over them with my fingertips. After a while, my stomach gurgles, reminding me that I haven't eaten since arriving on the ship.

"Come. Let's get you something to eat," Sara says as she rolls out of the bed. "We have a mess hall down the hallway. It's small, but it will do."

I get dressed and follow Sara into the mess hall. She wasn't kidding; it *is* small. It holds one table in the middle of the room, and a strange, white box in the corner. Is that some sort of intergalactic refrigerator? I sit down in one of the chairs while Wes and Aiden bicker in another room down the hallway.

"Are they going to be okay?" I ask as Sara makes her way over to the white square… block… thingy. She flashes me a tight smile.

"Of course, pet. Like I said before, they're working things out. They're probably just bickering over a television show they saw back on Earth, knowing them."

I laugh as I lean back in my chair. "Seriously? I didn't realize you three had time to get into human pop culture, what with everything else going on."

"Not much time, no. But what little time we did have, we devoted to learning as much of your culture as possible," she says.

The white block suddenly contorts itself into a small, rectangular object that looks more like a remote control for a television than anything else.

"What the hell?" I mutter as I watch Sara press several gray buttons. A tall glass of water materializes bit by bit on the table in front of me, along with a small blue capsule. I stare at both curiously.

"Oh. It's like in the shower, when you were asking Luci for things."

She nods and takes a seat across from me. "Yes. I'm still trying to work out how to move ourselves and other people, but I haven't perfected the system yet. It's going to take a lot more fiddling before I can beam us around."

I grin, then pop the capsule into my mouth and swallow it down with the glass of water. The cool sensation of the liquid hitting the back of my throat is blissful. I hadn't realized just how dehydrated I really was until now. The water is the sweetest I've ever tasted, too.

"Wow. Hey, wait. You mean you made that system?" I ask, impressed.

She nods with a bashful smile. "Yes. I created Luci. I'm very proud of her, though she still has a few kinks I need to troubleshoot. I'm getting there."

I nod. "I can relate. Every day in the office, it's like when we squash one bug, twenty more pop up."

Her laugh reminds me of a tinkling bell. It's beautiful, and my heart melts at the sound. "That's exactly my issue right now. It's going to take at least a month for me to get around to all the fixes I need."

She reaches across the table and offers me her hands, which I readily accept. She traces the back of my hands with her claws, and we sit in comfortable silence for several minutes. She's so lovely, especially in this form as her relaxed, genuine self. My cheeks burn when I think about all the salacious things we got up to in the shower just hours ago. Fuck, all I want to do is go back to that alien rainforest and have her order me around some more.

Wes storms into the mess hall. His gray skin is paler than usual, and his dark eyes flash from blue to red to black again. There's still so much about their anatomy I don't understand, and will probably never understand. He practically rips a free chair out from underneath the table and flops down onto it.

"I don't want to talk about it," he huffs.

Sara barely spares Wes a glance before pressing several buttons on the white controller.

"What can I get you, darling? Luci can create anything you'd like to eat. Wes, would you like something to eat as well?"

Wes shakes his head but doesn't say a word. I nibble my bottom lip while I watch him quietly stew in his own anger before answering. I'm starving, so right now anything sounds good.

"Pizza? I haven't had a decent slice in a while."

Living so close to New Jersey has me spoiled for good pizza, and I'm curious what her alien tech is capable of. She nods and presses a few more buttons before a slice of greasy, cheesy pizza forms in front of my very eyes on a white ceramic plate. The aroma of oregano and garlic is too enticing to ignore, and I dig in immediately. I let out a moan of pleasure as the tang of the tomato sauce hits my tongue. The way Wes jerks his head up to stare at me tells me I'm being downright pornographic about my food, but I don't care. I'm ravenous, and the pizza is gone within seconds.

Wes's tongue flicks across his bottom lip. I can't tell if he's aroused or hungry, and Sara laughs. "Would you like another?" she asks.

I shake my head. "No, thank you. Oh, but if you could conjure some long-hots for me, I'd be pretty psyched."

Sara blinks as she stares at me from across the table. "Long… hots?"

I smirk. "Sorry. Yeah, hot peppers. They're green, stored in garlic oil and—"

She doesn't wait for me to finish before pressing a few buttons on her device. Within moments, a pair of large, hot peppers appear on a plate. They look like the Italian peppers I'm used to, but do they taste correct? I reach for one and take a little nibble out of the end.

"How is it?" Sara asks as she leans against the table on her elbows. "I hope they're accurate."

I chew for several seconds before swallowing, then grab the glass of water to chase the heat down. "Whew. Those are delicious! And much hotter than I'm used to. Holy shit."

Wes stares at the lone pepper on the plate curiously, and I push it towards him.

"What? Oh, no. I couldn't. That's your pepper. Besides, I'm not sure if I can even safely eat that."

"Just try it," I say. He takes a deep breath and plucks the pepper from the plate, dribbling a little oil across the table. Then he mimics my pepper eating technique and takes a tentative nibble out of the end. He sets it down immediately and grabs my glass of water to wash it down. Sara laughs loudly, but I wince in sympathy as he's clearly struggling not to gag.

"Sorry, Wes. I shouldn't have insisted," I murmur.

"It's fine, it's fine," he says in between coughs. "But you eat this? For fun?"

I nod. "I do. I love them."

"I don't understand it, but I respect it," he says.

Sara nods with a soft smile. "Just let me know if you need anything else. We'll provide, or at least try to."

"Thank you. You've been so kind to me," I say. Wes's eyes flash from blue to black, and I can't help but smile.

"Why wouldn't we be? We like you," Sara says. Wes nods in agreement. "I've been meaning to ask, but haven't found the right time. Would you mind if I kept the data I collected from the probe? I could use it for my studies, but only with your permission, of course. Just say the word, and I'll destroy it. You'll never hear of this again."

Wes's eyes grow wider as he looks between Sara and I.

"Probe? You probed her?" he asks, surprised.

"In the shower, if you must know. Yes."

I take another crisp bite out of my hot pepper and smile. "I can't say I've ever been probed before, but I liked it. Sure, go ahead and use the data if it's helpful."

"Thank you, Taryn," she says.

I hesitate and look at Wes, who looks back at me with... sympathy? Tenderness? Something else entirely? I can't tell, because his bug-eyes don't exactly lend themselves well to human emotions.

"What were you going to use the data for, exactly?" I ask.

"I'm an engineer, but I also have a keen interest in human anatomy. Your species is relatively new to the rest of the universe, and I'd like to learn as much as I can. That's all."

It's strange having someone go up your vagina to collect data, but it's also Sara. I'm not as bothered by the idea as I probably should be.

"That's interesting. Well, let me know if you discover anything I should know about."

"Will do," Sara says before turning to Wes. "Where is Aiden?"

Wes emits a soft growl in agitation before saying, "In our quarters, sulking."

"Then I'm going to go check on him, if that's alright?" Sara looks back at me and smiles gently. "Please get some rest, and make sure you drink the rest of your water, sweet thing."

I can't help but notice she doesn't call me "pet" in front of Wes. I nod, and Sara leaves the mess hall in search of Aiden, leaving the two of us alone with one another. Again. I'm not sure what to say, because he doesn't seem up to talking. But I'm surprised when he puffs out his cheeks and leans towards me.

"So, the shower, huh?"

I nod as I blush fiercely. "Uh, yeah."

"I have to confess something."

As I wait for him to finish, I raise my eyebrows.

"I'm envious. I wish it was me in there with you," he whispers.

The idea of Wes and I alone in the showers together getting up to all sorts of mischief sounds…. great, actually. He notices the change in my demeanor and slides back into his seat.

"I shouldn't have said that," he says quietly.

"Why not? I would definitely be interested," I say. "I'm a little tired right now, and I need to drink my water, but… if you want, would you like to come back to bed with me? I can't promise anything, but—"

"Yes," he says, not letting me finish. "I would love to join you in bed. Even if all we do is cuddle. No expectations."

I drain the rest of my glass and offer him my hand. He wraps his black claws around my fingers carefully, as though afraid he might hurt me, and follows me back to my room. I don't hear any sound coming from down the hall, so whatever Sara and Aiden are up to, at least it's peaceful. Wes sinks down onto the edge of the bed and stares up at me, his eyes glossy and imperceptible.

"It's okay," I say as I run my fingertips along the sides of his face. He emits a small trill of pleasure in the back of my mind. Is he… purring? I'm not sure, but he doesn't tell me to stop. I place my hands on his thick, dark shoulders and push him back into the mattress. He props himself up against the mattress on his forearms and watches as I untie the front lace of my corset dress. When I let my dress drop to the floor in a pool by my feet, his mouth falls open.

"I thought we were just cuddling," he murmurs.

I grin as I take a step forward, then leap onto the bed to straddle him. The heat between my thighs is back. Normally, I'm never this horny. Sex twice a week is enough for me to feel satiated, but something's come over me. Ever since meeting my aliens—that's what I think I'll call them from now on—all I can think about is sex, and lots of it. Perhaps they had some sort of supernatural hold over me that I will never be able to comprehend, but in the end, it doesn't really matter. For the first time in a long time, I'm prioritizing my own pleasure, and damn, does it feel good.

"I guess I've changed my mind," I say as I run my hands across his gray chest. "Are you ready for me?"

"Yes," he whispers.

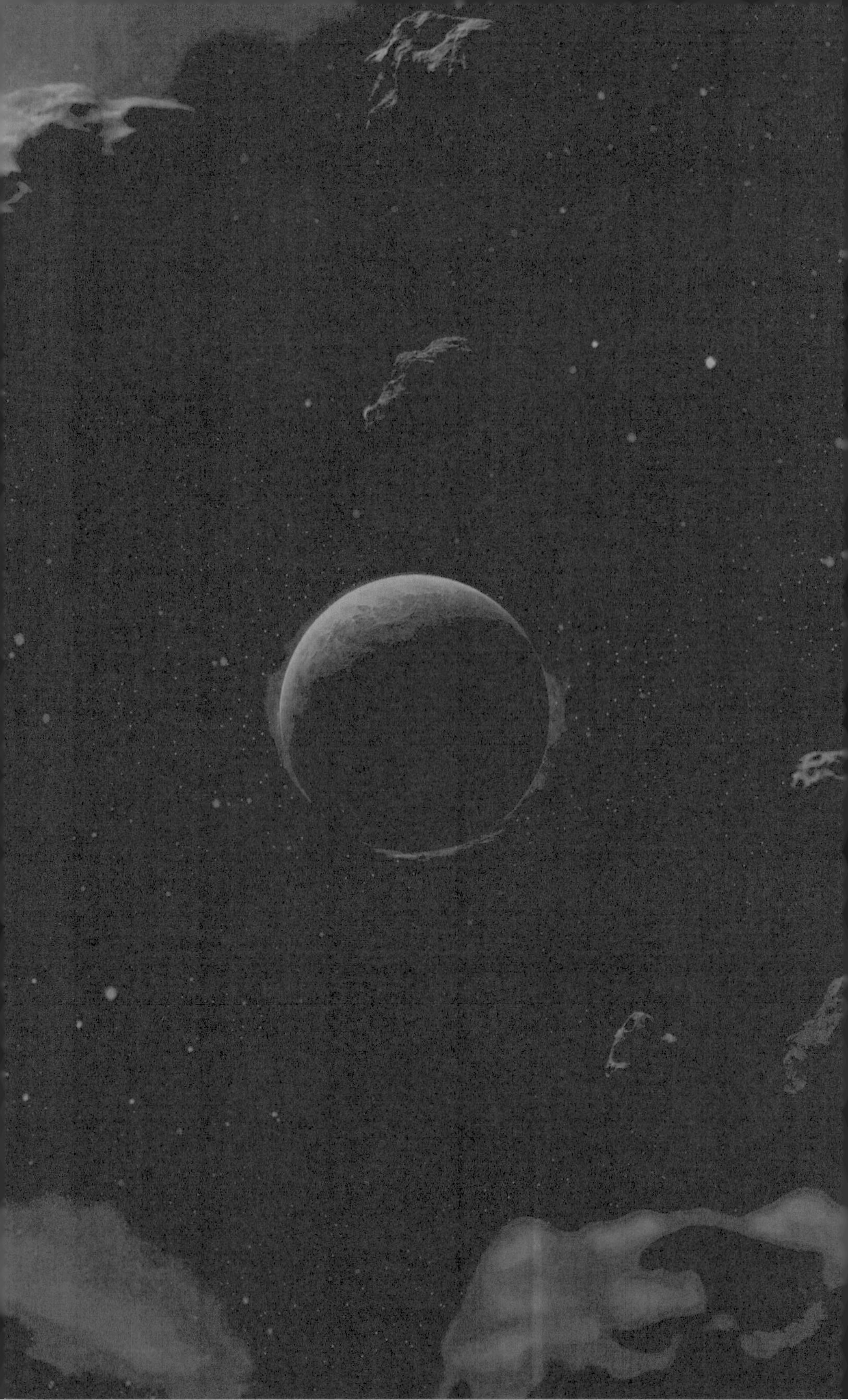

Chapter Thirteen

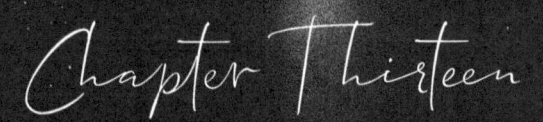

It's a good thing Wes can't actually cry out with his mouth, otherwise the entire ship would be vibrating right about now. This also means his cries and moans are directly inside my head, and I'll probably need to request a pain killer from Sara later. Oh, well. Totally worth the headache. The thing is, I haven't even really done anything to Wes to trigger this sort of reaction. I'm straddling his pelvis, sure, but…

"Taryn," he gasps in my mind. I look down at him and start to panic. Am I hurting him? Is he upset with me?

"Yes, Wes? Are you okay? Do you want me to stop?"

"No. But there's something you should know," he says so quietly I can barely make out his voice in my head. "I don't have a cock in this form," he says.

I bite my bottom lip as I grind my hips across his. I'm already slick with need. "Oh. Um, I figured it would be a *Shape of Water* situation and it was just… inside you, somewhere. You don't have one at *all*?"

He shakes his head. "No. Sorry."

I smile down at him and caress his face with my hands. He moans again, and I blink in confusion. "Okay, what am I doing that's causing you to make those noises, then?"

His eyes flash from blue to black again. "I get aroused by your arousal. It's a… sort of mate bond. When I'm bonded with someone in this form, I feel arousal and stimulation from my partner's pleasure."

"Are you serious?"

He blinks slowly as I roll off his body onto the soft blankets beside him. He groans in disappointment.

"That's amazing, Wes. I had no idea," I say. "How do we go about this, then? What would you like me to do?" I sit on my knees beside him, waiting.

"Let me worship you," he says. "Let me taste you, devour you."

My cheeks flood with heat, and before he can say another word, I'm pinning him on his back with his arms above his head. I've never been this aggressive before, but these aliens seem to be bringing out so many new sides of my personality I didn't know existed. Like I'm a trove of diamonds finally being unearthed after years beneath the dirt. His eyes flash as he stares up to watch me. He's patient, but I can hear him panting. Wes wants me, and without a cock, I'm going to have to get creative.

I do the only logical thing I can think of. I mount his face.

He moans in my mind, and he laps at my clit with the fervor of a starving animal being thrown a bone.

"Yes, Taryn, this is exactly what I was hoping for…" he says. When you don't need your mouth to speak, it makes face sitting a lot more convenient. He rakes his claws along my thighs and butt, and I place my hands against the wall firmly. "Fuck my face, Taryn," he pleads, and I oblige. I buck my hips back and forth in slow, rhythmic motions at first, giving him time to acclimate to my weight and movements.

"More," he begs.

The more I move against his mouth, the more he moans. And the more he moans, the harder he sucks my clit and the more my climax builds. The bed creaks beneath our shared weight, and I let loose a desperate moan as I shudder. I toss my hair behind my shoulders and work my cunt against his tongue.

"Yes, baby, that's so good," I purr. "I'm going to come soon."

His entire body goes rigid beneath me. My breasts bounce up and down as I fuck his face in sharp movements until finally the cord within my abdomen snaps and I scream.

"Yes! I'm coming!" I yell. He frantically moves his tongue in and out of me, taking those few extra moments to taste me before it's too late. When his own orgasm comes, I can feel it explode in my mind. Darkness sweeps through my senses, blinding me. I'm afraid at first until I realize I'm having another out-of-body experience like when Aiden fucked me against the wall. Gorgeous splatters of galaxies color my vision as I hurtle through the universe.

"Oh, stars…" I whisper. I reach forward to take hold of a star as I pass it, but then I'm tossed back into my body. When I come to, I'm on my back, staring up at the ceiling.

"Taryn? Taryn!" Wes shouts as he hovers over my body. "Are you okay?"

Am I okay? What kind of question is that? It feels like I'll never feel anything bad ever again.

"I'm perfect," I whisper in a hoarse voice. "Just perfect."

Chapter Fourteen

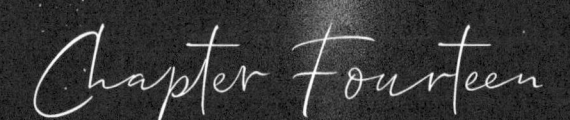

The next morning—or what I can only assume is morning—I wake to Wes's arms wrapped around me. He nuzzles into my neck, still fast asleep and dreaming. Wes snores through the tiny slits that make up his nose, and I can't help but giggle. It's too adorable.

"Wes," I mutter into his ear-hole.

"Mm?" He blinks open his eyes, and I smile at him.

"Good morning, sleepyhead. How'd you sleep?"

He groans in response. "Would have been better if a certain cute, little human hadn't just woken me up before I was ready," he says irritably. But I can tell he's not really annoyed with me. I shuffle beside him closer and press my lips against his.

"Wake up. I want breakfast," I mewl. "Please."

He huffs, but sits up and rubs the back of his head. "Since you said please, I guess I have no choice."

We get out of bed, and while he pads off to the mess hall, I get dressed. I really need a change of clothing, or at least a laundry machine, because my dress isn't smelling too fresh anymore. As I lace myself up, Aiden steps into the cabin in his human form.

"Hey?" I greet him, obviously confused.

He lifts his hand in greeting and smiles. "Hey. I just wanted to come by and check on you. Did you sleep well?"

I nod as I finish tying my corset. "Oh, yeah. Best rest I've had in ages, thanks to Wes. But why are you wearing that?"

He blinks and looks down at his shirt. "My t-shirt? It's cotton. I like cotton. It's breathable and soft."

I shake my head and laugh. "No, I meant your human form. What's up with that? You know I'm used to your other form, right?"

He smiles and shoves his hands into his jean pockets. "Oh. Right. I should've figured. Yes, I know. But I like taking this form. It's comfortable for me. I don't always choose my form because of others, you know. Sometimes I just like taking on different forms for the sake of it."

"That's fair," I say as I start to head towards him and the doorway. "Heard you and Wes arguing last night. Are you okay?"

He nods as he rubs the back of his neck. "We're good. Just a little disagreement over… you."

I pause in the doorway and look back at him. "Me?" I don't like the sound of that. There's nothing I want less than to come between a couple, and I frown.

"It's okay, trust me. He wanted me to try to convince you to stay with us. To be honest with you, I think… he's a little in love with you," he says as he closes the gap between us. He towers over me in this form, and I don't mind in the least. He looms over me and caresses the back of my head, stroking my hair. It's an intimate gesture, one I've come to cherish from the aliens. I swallow the lump in my throat as I consider his words. Wes is in love with me? My heart flutters at the thought.

"What are you thinking?" he asks.

I nibble my bottom lip and look up, allowing myself to get lost in his beautiful hazel eyes. "I'm thinking I don't hate the idea. And I really am into him, and you, for that matter. All three of you," I mutter, looking down at my feet. "I'm not used to this."

He stops petting my hair and inhales slowly. "What do you mean by 'this'? The polyamorous side of our relationship, or the fact that we're not the same species?"

"Both," I say. "Definitely both. I was raised in a conservative household. Which means my parents always assumed I'd get married to a man and pop out a couple of babies. The nuclear family thing, you know?"

He shakes his head. "I'm not familiar with the concept. We know a lot about Earth, but not everything. It doesn't help that you have so many cultures who practice different things. It makes learning… a lengthy and difficult process."

I nod. "Figures. Well, it's this idea that one man and one woman get together. They buy a big house, get a dog, and have children."

"What's wrong with that?"

"Nothing, it's just not for me. I don't want the whole relationship escalator thing. I'd prefer to try out different relationships the way I see fit, is all. I don't even *want* kids."

He chuckles and kisses the top of my head. "You're using some jargon I don't understand again, but I can comprehend the sentiment. I respect it. Loving multiple people isn't wrong, Taryn. It seems we might not have as many rules as your society in that respect. You could be very happy with us."

"Yeah. Well, I understand how he feels. I wasn't expecting to catch feelings after hooking up with the three of you, but… well, here we are. But I also told him I wanted to take things slowly."

Aiden draws another deep breath. "I know. He told me that, too. I said he should respect your wishes. He said he wanted to, but… Wes feels things very deeply. He's intense. He had a tough upbringing, and it makes him a little more desperate to hold on to the things and people he loves. Abandonment issues. But those aren't your responsibility. We're working through it together, he and I."

I smile. "I'm glad he has you."

"Me too. You were on your way to get breakfast, were you not? Don't let me keep you. I'll come along, too."

We head down to the mess hall, hand in hand. Sara and Wes are already at the table with stacks of pancakes on multiple plates. When I sniff the air,

I catch the sticky aroma of maple syrup and greasy, hot bacon.

"You three are spoiling me with these lavish meals. I don't know how I'm going to be able to go back to cooking on my crappy little apartment stove."

Wes looks down at the plate and goes still. Oh, shit. I probably shouldn't have said that. He's already feeling down about having to let me go. Sara stares at me as she holds up a plate of fluffy golden pancakes.

"Come eat before they get cold. I mean, I can always conjure more, but…"

I slide into a chair and pick up my fork and knife.

"Pass them over!"

The three of us inhale our pancakes and bacon, and when I'm finished, I feel so full I'll need to be rolled out of the room. I run my hands over my gut and loosen the laces on my corset to give my stomach more room. Sara laughs when she notices what I'm doing.

A chime overhead interrupts our digestion, and I flinch.

"Attention. Landing on the planet of Twyla in ten minutes. Please get to a secure area for landing. Attention. Landing on the planet of—"

"Yes, thank you, Luci!" Sara yells. "We got it."

My heart races as I look at each of their faces. We're landing. We're actually landing. Of course, I knew this would eventually happen. It had to, after all. But at the same time, I wasn't expecting my time aboard the ship to come to an end so soon. I'm not even sure how long I've been on the ship, if I'm being honest. It feels like days… but it could be weeks. Or months. I haven't been able to check because my phone died ages ago and I never bothered to ask if they had a power source I could use to recharge it.

"Well. Looks like we'll need to get ready for the descent. Wes, better get up to the bridge," Aiden says as he claps his hands on his knees, then stands up. "Taryn, could you head back to the cabin, please? We'll come for you when it's time to get ready."

"Of course," I say. As I head back to my room, my anxiety spikes.

Luci greets me the second I walk into the room.

"Welcome back, Taryn. Please have a seat on the bed."

I do as she instructs. It's not like an airplane, where I need to fasten my seatbelt and make sure my tray is in the upright position. This is all new to me. So, I pull my knees to my chest and bury my face in them, blocking out the light. And I wait.

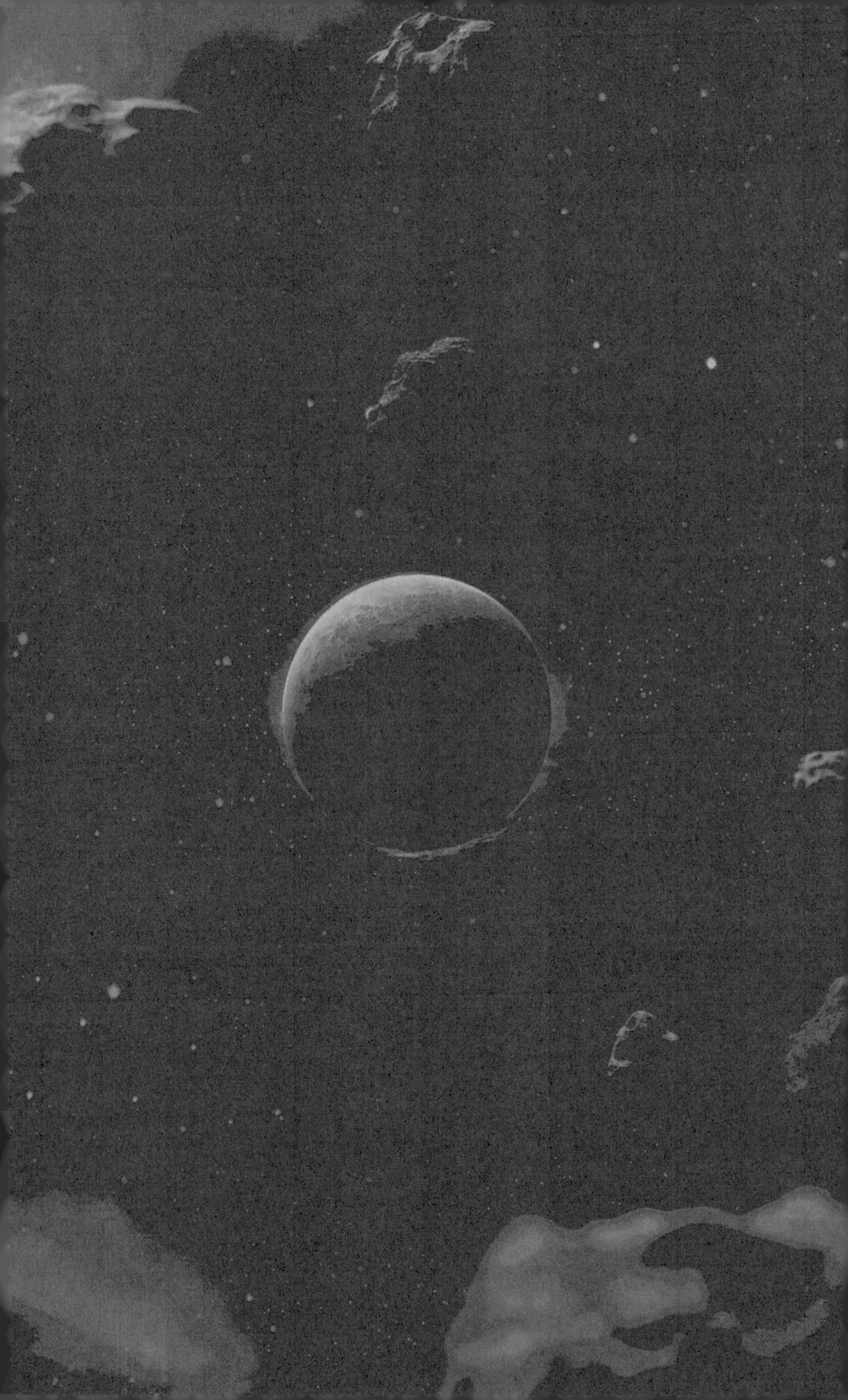

Chapter Fifteen

No matter how much deep breathing I do, I can't seem to calm down. The ship vibrates in a way it hasn't before, sending my imagination spiraling to all the worst-case scenarios I can think of. What if something is wrong, and the ship is about to disintegrate? What if there's a problem with landing, and we burn up in the planet's atmosphere, assuming it has one? There's still so much I don't know about their planet, and it's causing me to unravel.

I rock back and forth on the bed when the door to my cabin slides open and I look up to see Aiden step inside.

"Taryn? Taryn, are you feeling alright?" he asks as he approaches the bed. I'm shaking violently, unable to stop, and he clasps my shoulders in his hands to squeeze them. "Sweetheart. Look at me."

I'm panting so hard it feels like my heart is liable to burst at any moment. Am I dying? It certainly feels like it.

"You're having a panic attack," he says, then quickly sits down beside me. "It's going be okay. Everything is going as planned. Sara is one of the best engineers from the Academy, and Wes is a gifted pilot. They've done this thousands of times before. It's all routine. Just a few bumps while we enter our galaxy."

I nod. Rationally, I know he's right. There's nothing to be afraid of, because I trust them all with my life. So why won't my body believe it? He cups my face in his hands and presses his forehead to mine, then crushes my body against his chest.

"Let my heartbeat guide you," he murmurs. "Listen to my heart, and allow yours to match its rhythm."

I quiet the thoughts in my head just enough so I can listen to his heartbeat as instructed.

Badum.

Badum.

Badum.

His heart is a gentle drum, and the beating echoes in my mind until the blood in my veins finally slows. The nausea in my gut settles, and my heart begins to mimic his. I'm calm. When I pull back from his embrace, I smile at him. He returns the smile, though he also looks confused, like he's surprised his plan worked.

"Feeling better?" he asks. I nod. "Good, I'm glad. It hurt to see you in so much pain."

"Thank you," I say, and he kisses me on the forehead.

"Anything for you, Taryn."

And I believe him. Several minutes later, the intense vibrations turn into full-on shaking, and Aiden has me lie on my back as a precaution, just like when we went through the wormhole. While lying on his side, Aiden tells me stories of his childhood, what it was like growing up on Twyla as a boy, and his life as a young adult. I'm mesmerized as he regales me with tales of heartbreak and happiness.

"… So, as it turns out, Wes was at the bottom of the ravine waiting for the hunting party all along, but he had finished up hours before."

I cover my mouth as I laugh, enchanted by the story. "I never knew Wes was such a talented hunter."

He nods. "You'd never know it by speaking with him. He's always been the gentle one."

I lick my bottom lip and press my body against his, greedily taking as much of his warmth as his body will share with me. "Are you sure about that? Because I think you're pretty gentle, too, you know."

Aiden takes my wrist into his hand and pins it against the bed before kissing me long, deep, and hard. When he breaks the kiss, he looks deeply into my eyes before saying, "I can be gentle, but I'm known for my roughness as well."

A shiver runs down my spine as I press my hips against his. "Show me?"

The ship rumbles and quakes, but I barely notice it. I'm too busy kissing Aiden, and he's too busy running his hands up my and down my sides to care. He pushes his hands underneath the fabric of my dress and growls when his fingertips make contact with the tight corset.

"I want this off," he mutters. "Now."

He doesn't take his time removing my corset like Sara did, but he still takes care not to rip it. Once it's unlaced, he tosses it to the floor. Then he yanks down my skirt, panties, and bra until I'm completely naked. All of my clothing lands on the floor with a gentle thud, and he gropes my breasts in his palms and gives them both a gentle shake, feeling the weight of each.

"These are perfect," he murmurs before lowering his head down to suck on them. My nipples harden instantly into twin pebbles, and he removes his own shirt and tosses it aside to land with the other clothes. "But you've been getting a lot of attention lately, Taryn."

I blink as I stare at him, unsure of where he's going with that thought.

"And trust me, we've loved every moment of spoiling you." His mouth crashes against mine, and I moan into his mouth. He pulls back and draws in a breath. "I want you on your knees, sucking my cock," he says. His voice is firm, but not demanding.

"Is it safe?" I ask.

The ship rumbles from side to side in a gentle rocking motion. He pauses, then nods.

"Yes. If that changes, I'll let you know immediately," he says.

I roll off of the bed and drop down to my knees. Aiden swings his legs around to the side of the bed, unbuttons his jeans, and slides them down to the ground to reveal his black briefs. Those come off within seconds, too, revealing the hard length underneath. His cock is big, bigger than what I'm used to, but not so enormous his girth causes me pain. When he sits at the edge of the bed and strokes himself, he raises an eyebrow at me and sneers.

"Well? This cock isn't going to suck itself, as much as I wish it would," he teases.

I position myself between his thighs and lower myself over the tip of his cock. Tiny beads of pre-cum spill forth, and I push his hand away to grip his shaft. The pre-cum slickens the rest of his cock, and I tug and tease him, drawing out small growls and murmurs from his lips.

"Yeah, baby. That's good, keep it up," he moans in a raspy voice, and digs his fingernails into my scalp. I work his shaft with both of my hands at once, and he moans as I work them around his tip in slow, circular motions.

"Put those sweet lips of yours around the tip, baby. I want to know what the back of your throat feels like," he growls.

Of course, I oblige, and drag my tongue across his balls. I don't think he was expecting that, because his thighs twitch as he lets out a satisfied little moan. With my tongue I go around his tip in slow circles until he's panting and bucking his hips. I look up at him, meeting his intense gaze.

"Wes said that since you don't have cocks in your other form, you only become aroused by your partner's arousal. How does this work in your human form?" I ask, unable to keep my curiosity to myself. I have to know, even if it isn't the best time for questions.

He lets a low, throaty chuckle loose from deep within his throat and scratches my head. It feels good. And then he pulls my hair a little, and I gasp. Okay, now it feels *really* good.

"Different form, different anatomical needs. My cock works," he murmurs. "Why do you think I love this form so much?"

I raise an eyebrow and offer him a taunting smirk. "Ah, so you only like this form so much because of blowjobs?"

"Not only blowjobs. Sinking into your cunt up to my balls is a bonus, too."

"Is that a threat?" I ask, unable to keep the edge out of my voice. He glares at me and then stands up, pulling me along with him.

"You bet your sweet ass it is," he says, and then bends me over the bed. He slaps my ass with his palm and chuckles. "Luci, condom to cabin one, please."

I can hear the familiar crinkle of a condom from behind me, but I shake my head.

"We don't need it. I'm on birth control."

He laughs and pats my ass, gently this time. "Condoms aren't really necessary between our species, anyway. I can't impregnate you, and there are no transferrable diseases between our species."

Oh. Oh, wow. That's interesting.

"So, you were just using condoms before for show?"

"And to make you comfortable," he says. "Everything is for your comfort. You just tell me when you've had enough of me, sweetheart, and I'll turn down the temperature for you."

"You better not," I protest as I dig my fingernails into the blankets. He pulls my hair in response, and I let out a soft sigh.

"Good. Because I'm nowhere near done playing with you yet, and we still have some time before landing. Plenty of time," he purrs. I try to look over my shoulder at him, but he has my hair locked in his vice grip so I can't move my head. And then I feel his cock press against my entrance. I'm dripping with need, so lubricant isn't necessary this time. He presses his tip in between my folds, slowly at first, and I whimper.

"All good?" he asks.

"Mmhm."

He presses all of himself inside of me until I can feel his balls press against my skin. Oh, fuck. He feels almost too good. When he starts to move in and out of me in a gentle rocking motion, I lower myself down onto the bed on my forearms. This gives him a better angle, and he pushes himself even deeper into my depths. I bury my face in the sheets and let out a muffled cry. He bucks his hips faster and faster, and my heavy breasts sway from the motion. He drops my hair, letting it fall in a dark, wavy cascade across my back, then scoops my tits in between his palms.

He pinches my nipples between his fingers as he slaps against me, his powerful body persuading as much pleasure out of me as he possibly can.

"Oh, fuck!" I yell, and he squeezes my breasts in response. "I'm going to come!"

He chuckles, and when I look over my shoulder, I can finally catch a glimpse of him fucking me. His hard abs are drawn in tight, helping him with his rhythmic movements as he slides in and out of me. Aiden's length pulls out of me almost entirely before slipping it back inside between my folds, causing me to moan and writhe in his grasp.

"Let's go see some stars, babe," he says as he hovers over my back. Sweat from his neck slides down and drips onto the small of my back and down the outside of my thigh. My climax comes hard, and once again, I'm catapulted into that liminal space that seems to only exist when I'm orgasming.

Somewhere behind me, Aiden grunts as he comes in spurts. All the galaxies in the universe jumble together in my mind as I spin, spin, spin out of control until I'm slammed back into my own body. When I open my eyes, Aiden hovers above me, smiling.

"Welcome back, princess. Did you have a nice flight?" he asks.

"The best," I say, my cheeks flushed from satisfaction. I run my hand down my belly and between my thighs and snicker at just how… wet… everything is down there. "But now I feel like I need another shower."

He grins down at me and lowers himself to brush his lips against mine.

"I'll make sure you get your shower before you greet my people," he says, and I can't help but smile. He's been so sweet to me the past few days. It's hard to imagine a time when I didn't know him. Sometimes you meet someone new who just feels… *right*. Who feels like you've been friends for decades instead of days.

"Thank you," I mouth silently and roll into his side. He wraps his arm around my middle and pulls me into a warm embrace. I nuzzle my nose into his chest and sigh until my curiosity gets the better of me. There's something I've been meaning to ask him, but just haven't found the right time.

"Hey," I say into his chest, my voice muffled. "Can I ask you something?"

"Anything," he replies, then kisses the top of my head. My heart doubles over from the sweet gesture, and I pull away from his chest to look up into his hazel eyes.

"What's your real name? It can't be Aiden. Sara is Sarannia, and Wes is… Wesli—" I stop as I try to remember the rest of his name. It's too long, and I trip over the syllables. Aiden chuckles.

"Wesliannikos, yeah." He takes a deep breath, then lowers his lips to my ear, like I'm about to be privy to a closely guarded secret. "My name… is Aiden."

I roll my eyes and smack him in the arm.

"Come on, be serious," I say.

"I am! It's actually Aiden. If we're getting technical about it, my name is spelled a lot differently from how it's spelled on Earth. It's A-den. A hyphen between the A, no i, then den."

I stare up at him with a tight smile. "You're not fucking with me, are you?"

He shakes his head and laughs again. "No! I promise, I'm not. It means steward in our language. I take that role seriously, by the way."

"I can tell," I say before burying my face into his chest again. "Well, thank you for telling me. Sorry for all the questions."

He strokes my hair, and I practically melt into his muscular frame. Being in his arms like this is as close as I'm going to get to pure bliss.

"Princess, you can ask me all the questions you want," he whispers into my ear, and I drift off into a peaceful slumber.

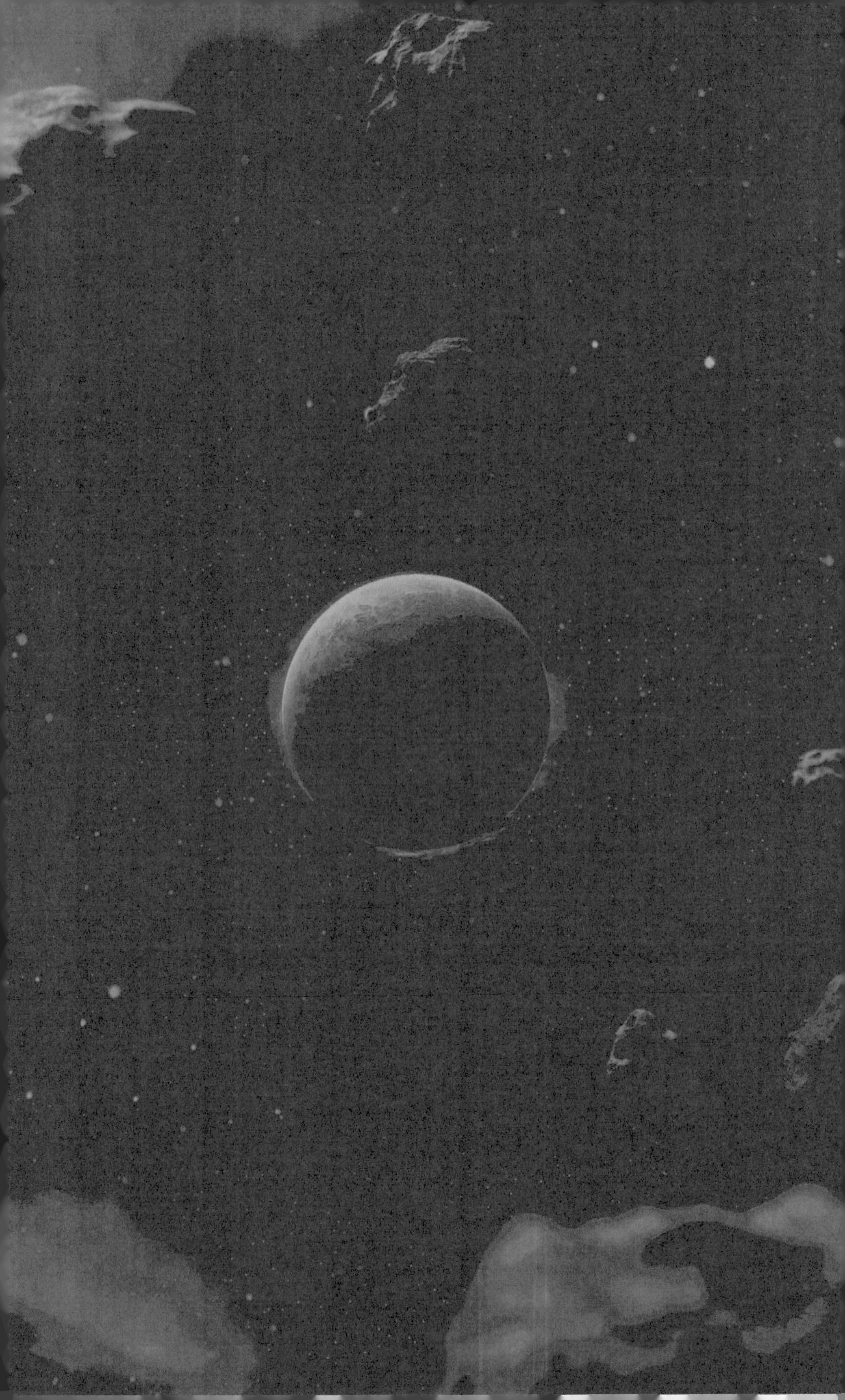

Chapter Sixteen

After my shower, I head back to my cabin to wait for my aliens to come get me. There's still so much to do in preparation for the landing, and I don't want to get in their way. But waiting around and staring at the blank walls is boring, so I decide to trawl my various social media feeds while everyone on the ship prepares for my grand debut into Twyla society. Sara was kind enough to charge my phone while Aiden and I spent time together, and I can finally see how much time has really passed back home. Evidently, I've only missed three days on Earth. Absolutely wild.

Thanks to interstellar internet, or whatever the fuck it's called, I'm able to send a text to Amber letting her know I'm okay, but that I'm just sick from the con crud. I don't need her popping over to my place only to find me missing. I also let the office know I wouldn't be in for at least a week. I don't think they'll even notice my absence, if I'm being honest with myself.

As I snuggle into the blankets of my bed, my phone dings with a notification from NewTube:

"Heard you got con crud. @AmberRose227 told us! Feel better!"

Sweet, wonderful Amber. She's always got my back. Probably figured I wouldn't be able to handle the stress of keeping up with my accounts while sick and told everyone where I was. I miss her. I wish I could show her all the miraculous things I've seen, but I know I can never tell her. As much as Amber loves me, asking her to suspend disbelief that much is a no-go. She'll think I'm having a nervous breakdown and make me go for a psych evaluation, and I wouldn't blame her one bit.

"Luci, can you turn the lights down to five, please?" I ask overhead as I press my back against the fluffy white pillow. As much as I'm looking forward to fresh air and sunshine, I'm going to miss this bed. It's been a godsend for my back. I don't think I've had a single body ache since sleeping on this mattress. I wonder if the aliens would let me take it with me back to Earth?

"Command accepted, Taryn," Luci replies. The lights lower to a dusky brown, just dark enough for me to fall asleep, but not so dark I can't see where I'm going in case I need to pee.

I know it's only been a few days, but I've adjusted to life in space. Not like it's been hard. Three square meals a day followed by hours of the most sensual, satisfying sex I've ever had makes me want to stay aboard for the rest of my life. But I know eventually it will end. It has to. I can't hide away like an actual pet forever.

Luci's chimes ping into the room, and I set my phone down to pay attention to her impending announcement.

"Greetings, Taryn. The captain wishes for me to inform you of our impending arrival. We will be entering the atmosphere momentarily."

My heart canters in my chest. Oh, shit. We're landing? I leap out of the bed and grab my underwear from the floor and pull it on as quickly as I can. The door slides open, and Aiden steps in. He's in his gray form, but I don't mind. He'll always be handsome to me, no matter what form he chooses to take.

"Ah, good. Luci told you. I came to give you the rundown of what's going to happen."

I nod. "Um, before that... who exactly is the captain? Is it Wes?"

Aiden's gray skin blanches as he blinks. "Oh." His tongue flicks against his bottom lip. "I am. We never told you?" He scratches the back of his head, looking positively sheepish. "I'm sorry. That's rude of us. Okay, so like I said before, Wes is our pilot, Sara is our engineer. I'm the captain. The ship's only big enough to accommodate four people; otherwise, we'd probably have proper medical staff."

It all makes perfect sense to me now. Aiden as the captain, with his gentle yet firm nature calling the shots and making sure everything goes according to plan. My face flushes as I recall the way he took control in bed, and the sound of his growl when he told me to suck his cock. This was a man who knew what he wanted in life, and just how to get it.

"Taryn. Taryn, focus," he says. I snap back to attention and find Aiden standing only a couple inches in front of me. My imagination got the better of me again, but this was hardly the time for it.

"Sorry. I was daydreaming again, I think."

He chuckles. "It's alright, just... this next part is important, and I want to make sure you're paying attention. We're going to land. We have a special suit for you, but our atmosphere is almost identical to Earth's so you probably won't need it. Until the medical staff at the facility can take some tests and give you the all-clear, do not remove any part of your suit."

I nod. "I can handle that."

"Good."

He strokes my arms up and down, then turns to head back out the door. I watch him go, and Sara appears in the doorway seconds later, clutching the white suit in her arms. I'm not sure what I expected, but it definitely wasn't spandex. Sara smiles when she sees the bewilderment on my face and holds the suit up, allowing it to unravel. I grimace as I flick my gaze up and down the length of the suit, taking in the tackiness of it. Yup, that is definitely spandex.

"I'll help you get into it. Don't worry, it's very comfortable," she says as she smooths out a crease on the front.

No doubt, considering it looks like skin tight pajamas. It sucks that I have to wear this just to be introduced to their community, but I've worn worse to Halloween parties, I remind myself.

After several minutes of wriggling into the damn thing, I'm ready. I'm glad there aren't any mirrors inside the cabin, or else I'd probably get cold feet. I'm already starting to regret my life choices, and I flap my arms up and down at my sides before releasing a long, discontented sigh.

"You're not wearing it to make a fashion statement. You're wearing it to not die," Sara says firmly. She's a lot more patient with me than she probably should be right now, and I adore her for it. I groan. She's right, of course. I can't be silly about this.

"I know. I just wish I could at least make a better impression, is all. I feel like I'm Mike Teavee getting ready to jump into Wonkavision."

She takes a step forward and curls herself around me in a protective hug. Her body is so slender, so soft compared to Aiden's.

"What better impression could you possibly make? You're here to save lives. That's good enough, Taryn. No one cares what you look like. You are good enough and always have been."

I raise an eyebrow and snort before looking down at myself again. She was right. It is very comfortable. "You're probably just saying that because I have the right blood type," I mumble.

Sara runs her claws across my scalp and squeezes me tighter. "I'm saying it because you're Taryn. Do you really think we'd go through all this trouble to bring you back with us, a whole human, because of your blood type?" She pulls me away to look me in the eye. "Trust me. If we didn't like you, we'd have moved on to the next city. And then the next, until we did find a human worth bringing along. It's too long of a trip to be stuck with someone we didn't like."

My heart flutters again, and I can't help but smile. My cheeks burn. I'm not used to receiving such sweet compliments, such adoration. It's been a lot to adjust to.

"That's a good girl." She kisses me on my cheek, then my forehead. "Forget Mike Teavee. You would make a very adorable Oompa Loopma, my sweet. Orange is your color."

"Orange is no one's color," I say. "Also, I didn't know you saw *Willy Wonka*."

She nods as her smile forms a tight line. "I did, and I hated it. Such a weird film. What fucked up things that man did to those children. Anyway, let's get going, pet."

She swats me on the butt before we head out the door.

"Ready to go, space cadet?" Wes winks at me as he walks past, eager to get off the ship as much as the others. Clad in my spandex suit and mesh hood—I have no idea how this is supposed to keep me alive, but whatever—I stand in front of a heavyset door that I assume says, 'DO NOT OPEN UNLESS YOU WANT TO DIE A HORRIBLE DEATH.' But since I can't read whatever alien language is written on it, I can only speculate.

"Yeah. Ready as I'll ever be, I guess," I say with a limp shrug. Adrenaline has been coursing through my veins for so long I forgot what it felt like to ever be at ease. Was I ever calm and collected?

Wes pats me on my shoulder and blinks at me slowly, exactly three times. I've come to learn that's his way of showing affection, like a cat. I turn to face him and blink back, except he can't see it thanks to the mesh.

"Thank you," I murmur. He leans forward and presses his forehead against mine. Or at least, he tries to. It's the thought that counts, right?

"For what?"

"For going slow with me. For being my friend. For everything, I guess," I say.

He reaches around my waist and lifts me off the ground.

"You don't have to thank me for that. It comes with the territory of being in my family."

My heart warms, but there's no time for me to swoon. The doors open with a hydraulic hiss, and I step behind Wes. Sara rushes forward, eager to be the first one off the ship. Aiden clears his throat as he steps behind me.

"It's going to be okay. They won't harm you," he says quietly. I nod. I trust him. I trust all three of them, a thought I would have considered ridiculous up until recently. Life has a way of surprising you when you least expect it.

The doorway slides out and upward with a strange whirring noise until it finally stops. Light filters into the room, and I shield my eyes. Despite the mesh, it's difficult to see thanks to the triple suns hanging in the sky.

"You didn't tell me you had three suns," I say in annoyance.

"We don't. Those aren't suns. Well. Two of them are. One of them is another planet. It's just bright as fuck," Wes quips.

"Still."

Dozens of dark bodies huddle together in a crowd. I can't make out any details, only their silhouettes. They're tall, thin, and moving towards the doorway. My heart races as I begin to sweat in my suit. Oh, god. What if they hate me? What if this is all a ruse, and my aliens actually did kidnap me after all for some freaky experiments? My vision swirls and I start to feel lightheaded until Wes takes one of my hands and tugs me forward. Aiden takes the other, and they flank my sides, leading me down the ramp into the bright sunlight.

A fresh sea breeze fills my lungs, and the tinkling of little birds chirping fills my ears. My senses come alive as the planet greets me. The dark figures finally come into focus, and I start to make out their individual features. Dozens of people gather around us. Some look like Aiden and Wes, and a couple look just like Sara. Others look nothing like my aliens, with horns jutting from their skulls in gnarled twists that remind me of gazelles and rams from Earth. Some are more serpentine in nature, forgoing legs entirely. As their curious eyes search me, I swallow the bile that rises in the back of my throat.

I can't do this.

I can't do this.

I can't—

"Greetings, human! Welcome to our home," a voice cries out in the back of my mind. I blink back tears in surprise. "You are welcome here."

Oh. They speak English. How… unexpected. A pair of gazelle-like aliens move forward to bow before me. I'm not sure what to do, and peer up at Aiden for help.

"You can bow back if you want to," he says and he rests his hand on my shoulder.

I bow, because it seems like the polite thing to do. The aliens murmur in keen interest as they flock around us excitedly. Sara moves amongst the crowd, hugging and kissing her friends. Some of the aliens sob, while others laugh. My terror ebbs away little by little and is replaced with a creeping anxiety that threatens to turn into yet another panic attack. Oh, please. Not here, not now. Aiden's voice brings me back, centering me, and I'm grateful for his presence.

"Everyone, this is Taryn," Aiden says as he claps a hand on my shoulder. Wes wraps his arm around my waist protectively. "And she's here to save us."

"No pressure or anything," I mutter through one of the corners of my mouth.

A chorus of happy cries erupt in the air. The wind pushes me forward, and I am immediately taken into the loving arms of the aliens. My anxiety melts away as they lead me down the grassy hill, and it's then that I notice the plants here are purple instead of green. The sky is orange instead of blue, and a city the color of steel sits nestled between twin mountains covered in snow.

I'm not sure where this adventure will take me, but wherever I'm going, at least I won't be alone. A girl no taller than my waist approaches me and holds her hand up for me to take. She's covered head to toe in dark feathers, and when I reach down to take her hand, bird-like claws lace between my fingers. I smile at her, and she smiles back. Whatever doubts I had before have floated away, like the tide drifting back to sea.

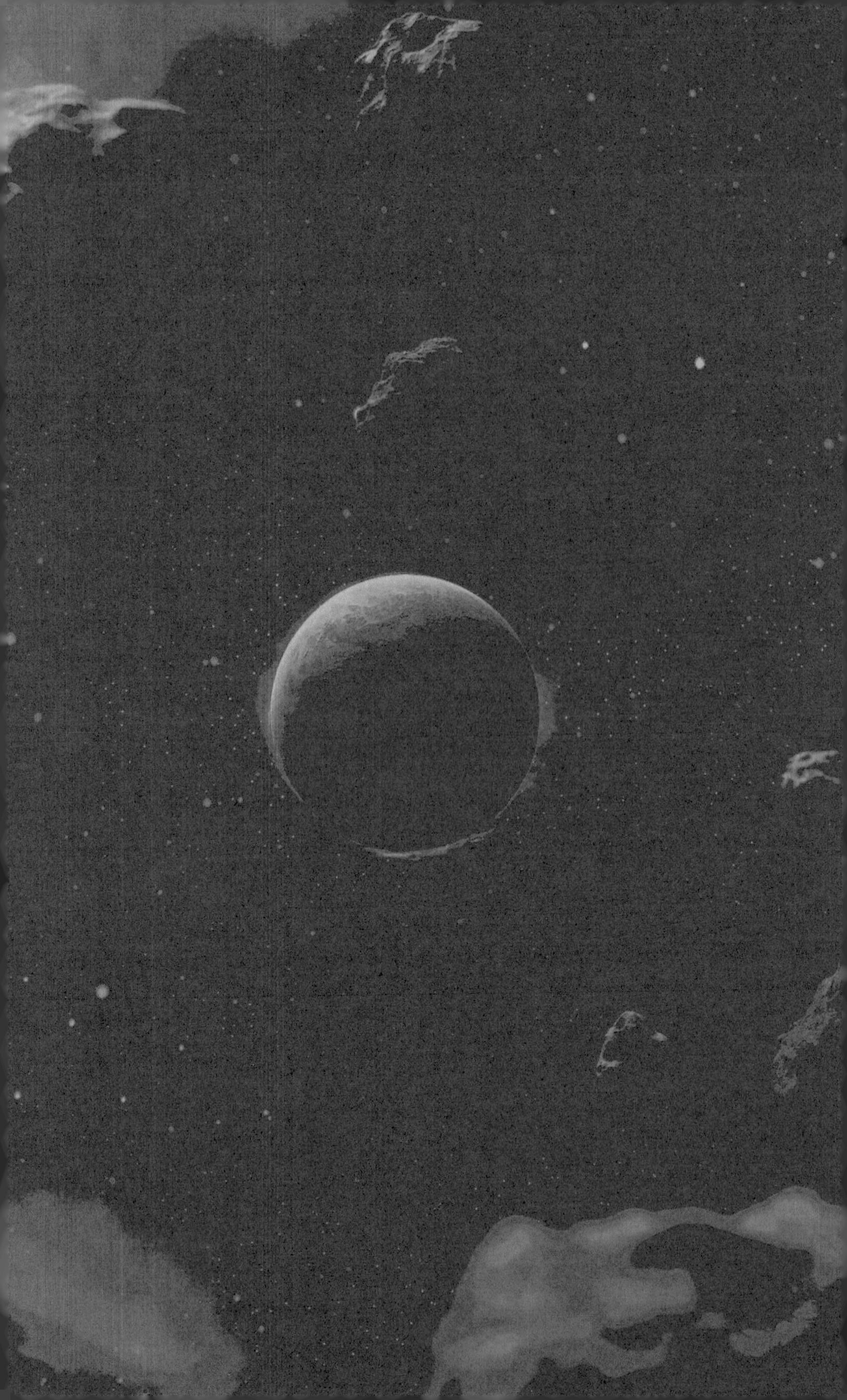

Epilogue

ONE YEAR LATER

"Hey, Taryn? I need you to take a look at this when you have a chance." Mike, my supervisor, sends along a file through the company group chat as he passes by my desk. I groan when I open the file and notice the million bugs almost immediately.

"Mike, seriously? This is going to take an extra five hours to get through. You can't be serious. It's Friday," I say.

Mike shrugs and doesn't even look up at me. He's too busy scrolling through his social media to bother. I slump back against my chair as I wait for him to say something—anything—but he doesn't. I really need to quit. Why haven't I quit yet?

I check the calendar. It's August 26th, and it is one week away from Chimera Con. I just have to get through this last week of work, and I'll finally be free of responsibilities. For a few days, at least. Sandra, the only co-worker in the whole office who I actually like, spins by my desk to deliver a cup of freshly roasted coffee. The aroma perks me up the second it hits my nostrils, and I smile.

"Mm, thank you so much. You always know exactly what I need," I say. Sandra smiles and does a little curtsey in front of my desk.

"Excited for the weekend? You and Amber rooming together again?" she asks.

"Yeah. I don't think I'll see her all that much, though. She's got plans with her girlfriend all weekend long. What about you? Got anything exciting planned?"

Sandra shakes her head and runs her fingers through her freshly cut bob. "Nah. Me and Mark are gonna stay in and marathon some horror movies. But you're going to be all alone again? What's up with that?"

I look back at the computer screen and sigh.

"No, not alone. I'm meeting a few friends, I think."

She raises her own mug to her lips and lofts a brow. "You think? So… it's not a definite thing?"

"Not a definite, but I'm hoping everything pans out."

Sandra nods slowly as she starts walking back towards her desk. "Well, for your sake, I hope so, too."

As if I didn't have enough to worry about with work, now I'm freaking out whether they're going to actually show up or not after all. My gut wrenches as I inhale the scent of freshly brewed coffee, remembering how the three used to guzzle it down like it was water.

A year ago, my entire life changed when I met three aliens masquerading as humans over Labor Day weekend. I traveled across the stars to cure their people of a deadly disease, made new friends, and made promises I intended to keep. The Twyla—the name for Aiden and Wes's people, after their home planet, I came to learn—were able to replicate my blood cells successfully. They created a cure for the disease that ravaged their population for years, and finally, their people were able to live their lives without fear. I was happy for them, of course. Especially Wes, whose little sister made a full recovery before I left for Earth. They had their lives back, which also meant they didn't need me anymore. I was free to go back home.

Of course, my aliens didn't actually say that. They wouldn't. But it sure as hell felt like no one needed me around anymore once the last blood bag was filled.

They wanted me to stay, but I couldn't just up and abandon my life here on Earth. I had Amber, my parents, my job. Aside from spending my days with my aliens, what else could I do? They understood and respected my decision to return, despite being gutted by that choice. But I couldn't just run from one relationship to another, especially when it meant relocating to a whole new planet in another universe. Try explaining that one to friends and family.

And of course, the second I got back to my apartment in Philly, the men in black paid me a little visit. They were just as terrifying as everyone made them out to be, by the way, only worse. Their skin looked like plastic and they were both at least six-foot-five. They threatened to have me "disappeared" off the face of the Earth should I tell anyone about my little off-world adventure. They also made me put an end to my NewTube channel, which meant no more ad revenue. That part stung. I really needed that money, and now that it was gone? I had to move to a smaller apartment outside of the city, which meant my commute was crap. But hey, at least I still had a job. A job that I hated, but a job nonetheless. Life went on. I went to work, I spent time with my friends and family, and I never heard from Brandon again after last year's Con, just as he promised. It's funny how life changed so quickly, and yet it felt like everything was still the same in so many respects. Though I didn't miss Brandon, not even a little, there was a large alien-shaped hole in my heart.

Before I left Twyla, the three of us made a pact: one year from now, if everyone was still on board with the idea, we'd meet up at the next Chimera Con. I would get the space I needed to grow outside of a relationship, and my aliens would devote themselves to their people's recovery. It made sense for all four of us, but it didn't feel great. In fact, it sucked. Hard.

I tossed and turned in bed for twelve months as I agonized over the worst-case scenarios. What if they didn't show up? What if they forgot about me and moved on with their lives?

It was a special kind of torture that kept me from fully moving on, and it was completely self-inflicted. After all, I was supposed to be learning how to live on my own without Brandon. And I did that. Every meal I made, every load of laundry I did, every errand I ran was for me. I fell into a comfortable routine of taking care of myself, calling my parents, and going on weekly coffee dates with Amber. All in all, I was doing okay at life. But despite doing everything well on paper, it still felt like I was missing something.

An entire year later, I realized I no longer missed the ambiguous idea of a relationship anymore. I missed Aiden, Wes, and Sara. I yearned for them, especially at night when I was alone in my bed and all I had to keep me company were my own thoughts. I wanted to touch them, kiss them, tell them about my day. Complain to them about work. I wanted to hear them talk about their own lives, what their hopes and dreams were for the future. Normal relationship stuff.

If they returned to Earth, I decided I would go with them. For good this time. I was ready. But until then? I still had to work, just in case they didn't feel the same way.

Two hours later, Mike paces in front of my desk with a stack of papers in his hand.

"Please don't say those are for me. Mike, come on," I plead as I watch him toss the stack down onto my desk.

"Sorry, Taryn. You're the only one who can get this done on time! We need you."

Why did that sound so familiar? This company needs me like… a fish needs a bicycle. Fuck.

I roll my eyes. "The only reason I get things done on time is because you let everyone else in the office fuck around. Dave is over there on his Facebook, for crying out loud."

Mike looks over his shoulder at Dave and glares at him, but Dave doesn't so much as flinch. He just keeps on scrolling down his feed with a glassy-eyed stare.

"Give it to someone else," I say firmly.

Mike groans and runs his palm down his face. Here comes the guilt trip.

"Taryn, you're a real team player. That's why we like you so much. But if this doesn't get done, we won't make our deadline. I just need you to look over a few th—"

My chair screeches in protest as I stand up.

"You know what, Mike? No. I'm done. I told you three weeks ago at the meeting I was burnt out. You said 'oh, sucks' and patted me on the head. Literally. Which is all sorts of fucked up, by the way. I'm out. Find someone else to do this for you," I say, and then turn on my heel to make a beeline for the door.

Mike sputters and chokes on his coffee, then slams his mug down onto the desk before chasing after me.

"Wait, Taryn! Stop, please. Don't do this, we need you. Seriously—"

I spin around and glare at him. "Then you should have given me that raise I wanted, given me my vacation time, and taken my complaints seriously. Goodbye, Mike. Good luck to you."

I head out the door, my heart pounding in my ears, not looking back even once before stepping into the elevator. I did that. I really did that. And damn, did it feel good.

"So, you chose the nuclear option," Amber says as she stirs a dollop of honey into her tea. Amber dropped everything and ran across the city the second I hit 'send' on my text, declaring I had just quit my job in the most spectacular fashion. We headed to the nearest café to grab pastries, my go-to food item of choice in a crisis.

"Yup," I say as I cram another cinnamon roll into my mouth. "Sure did."

Amber stares at me from across the table. I know what she's thinking. She's thinking I've lost my damned mind. But I've never felt freer in my whole life, so I know I must've done something right. It's about time I prioritized my mental health. It just sucks that she can't see that this was something that needed to happen for a long, long time.

"I know, I know," I begin. "But listen, I was miserable over there for years. And it's not like I didn't talk to Mike about it. I did. Repeatedly. Nothing ever changed."

Amber nods as she pours a packet of sugar into her tea. "I know. I'm just worried, is all. What are you going to do now? You should have given them more notice than that. Now it's going to look shady on your resume."

I sigh as I slump back into my chair. I hate how she's always right. The corporate world sucks. Why did I ever think being a data analyst was worth the stress? Oh, right. Because of the money. Yeah, the money was good, but it wasn't worth my sanity. What I need is a change. A clean, hard break. Something new and exciting to get me out of bed in the morning.

"I'm going to switch careers."

She stares at me, wide-eyed and slack jawed. Amber loosens another packet of sugar into her tea, and then another. I put my hand on top of hers and shake my head.

"Amber, do you want any coffee with that sugar?" I tease.

Amber swallows hard as she stares at me. I can't joke myself out of this one. Not this time.

"You're thirty-one," she says in a monotone.

"And?"

Amber groans as she clangs her metal spoon around in her mug, and I wince. "And isn't it a little late in the game to be switching career paths?"

I snort and lean against the table on my elbows. Outside, it starts to rain. People on the sidewalk pull out their umbrellas while others run for cover. Autumn is starting early this year, it seems. Not that I'm complaining. The chill in the air reminds me that it's almost time for Chimera Con. I roll my eyes before taking a sip of my own drink. It's bitter, and I realize too late I forgot to put any sweetener in it. I cringe as I set the mug down, my hand trembling. A few brown droplets escape the mug and splatter onto the table.

"I'm not dead, Amber. That's such a cynical view. No, I'm not too old. Thirty-one is still considered young, you know. I bet I could go back to school, study something different. Maybe try my hand at astronomy."

She reaches across the table and places her hand on top of mine. Her touch is meant to be soothing, but I can't help but pull away as she asks, "Is this some sort of midlife crisis? Ever since you and Brandon split, you haven't exactly been yourself."

Ever since Brandon and I split, I've felt more like myself than I have in years. It's too bad my best friend can't seem to realize that, but that's not fair of me, either. It's not like I could tell her about Twyla, its people, or the men in black. She still thinks I shut down my channel because of a mental health crisis, too, and not because I was literally forced into giving it up.

I shake my head, letting my dark hair fall into my eyes.

"Amber. Please try to trust me on this one. I'm feeling… great. It's like a weight's been lifted from my chest. I couldn't breathe in that job. It was suffocating me. I was crying every morning before having to go in."

Her bottom lip quivers for a few seconds, then she nods. "Okay. I trust you. And I'm here for you, every step of the way. You have my support."

Finally. I was really starting to worry she was going to mother me more than my own mother.

I flash her a genuine smile and say, "Thank you. That's all I really wanted. Now, come on. Let's talk about your costume for this weekend."

Later that night, Amber and I curl up on the couch together to watch James Cameron's *The Abyss*. It's one of my all-time favorite movies, but it hits harder now that I've actually been to a real, live alien world. Instead of feeling thrilled when Bud walks out of the alien ship at the end, I just feel a sense of melancholy. Amber senses the change in my mood and hands me the box of tissues from the coffee table.

"Hey, are you okay? Do you have something you need to talk about? Is it the job thing? It might not be too late to ask for it back."

I shake my head as I dab at my eyes. Dammit. I wasn't expecting to get all teary-eyed in front of her. "No. I'm fine," I lie.

The truth is, I haven't been fine for a while, because I left my heart behind on a strange planet and I have no clue if I'll ever get it back. Is this how it's always going to be from now on? I'll see a movie about aliens and just burst into tears? It sounds ridiculous, but I might have to prepare myself for that possibility. Amber finally heads home, but it takes a lot of reassurance that I won't spend the rest of the night crying into my pillows. I wander into the kitchen, pour myself a nightcap of whisky, and nurse it while I lean against the cabinets.

I put my empty glass into the sink, and I'm about to head to the bedroom to get some much-needed shut eye when I notice a faint vibration beneath my feet. At first, I assume it's someone's stereo blaring too loudly. It's a Friday night, after all, and I have younger neighbors who love to party every weekend. But then the vibration is accompanied by a familiar, low hum. My heart leaps into my throat as I rush to the balcony. I yank open the doors and step out onto it and look around.

All I see are trees. Trees, shrubs, and darkness. Okay, now I'm hearing things. My imagination is running wild again, and I'm experiencing auditory hallucinations.

"Of course not…" I whisper to the wind, and I lean against the iron railing with a soft sigh.

"Of course not, what?" A deep, masculine voice says from behind me. I whirl around and stifle the urge to scream. Standing in the middle of my living room wearing a pair of dark-washed jeans and a white t-shirt is Aiden, looking like he just stepped out of one of my daydreams.

"A-Aiden?" I stammer as I place a hand on my chest. My heart is beating so fast, I'm worried I'll end up passing out from the shock. It's happened before. For someone who's literally been to space and probed, it's strange that I still have the constitution of a field mouse.

Aiden takes a step forward and grins. "It's me. Sorry for suddenly appearing in your living room like this. I let myself in. I made sure your friend left first, though. But damn, I thought she'd never go home."

"B-but how?" I step forward and nearly stumble over the raised entryway. Aiden hurries forward to take me by my forearms, and guides me into the living room.

"I just beamed myself in from the ship, princess," he says as he holds up his wrist to show off a silver, watch-like device.

Wait, beamed himself in from the ship? But that wasn't possible, I didn't think. Sara. Her experiments and hard work must have finally paid off!

"She did it? Sara finally did it?!" I jump up and down and throw my arms around Aiden's neck. He laughs at my excitement and brushes his nose against mine.

"Yes. She finally did it. She's been beaming us around all over the place for a week now. It's getting kind of annoying, if I'm being honest. She'll even beam us into the kitchen just to fetch her a snack when she's working. Seriously, she needs to be stopped."

I tilt my head as I study his face. He's still as handsome as ever, and I can't help but caress his cheek with my thumbs. My thoughts then drift to the others.

"Where are they? Wes and Sara?" I look around wildly, as though expecting them to suddenly leap out of my storage closet. Aiden strokes my hair and chuckles.

"They're back in the ship. They didn't want to overwhelm you, so they sent me in first. Feel you out, see if you were… home." He glances around my apartment carefully, as though looking for something. Or someone.

"It's just me who lives here," I say. "No roommates or anything, so we won't be interrupted."

His cheeks color, and I grin. "Are you blushing? You just said you waited for Amber to leave. But were you expecting someone else?"

Aiden brushes his knuckles against my cheek and smiles. "I was hoping you weren't attached to someone else, as selfish as that is. I couldn't be sure. It's been a year for you, and you're quite the catch, after all. I figured someone would've scooped you up by now."

I roll my eyes. Yeah. Fat chance of that happening. If only he knew just how much I missed him. All three of them.

"And how long has it been for you? Two whole seconds?"

He shakes his head. "A couple of months. Which… trust me, is long enough. We've missed you so much. Wes kept trying to talk us into checking on you sooner, but we made a promise, and we don't break our promises."

"I've missed you, too. All three of you." I wrap myself around his torso in a tight, desperate hug full of longing and a year's worth of love. He runs his palm across my head as I cling to him, too afraid to let go. What if I passed out on the couch and this is all just a dream? If I pinch myself, will I wake up on the floor, alone? I force back tears as I bury my face into him.

"Please be real," I murmur against his warm chest.

The chuckle in his throat sounds more like a deep rumble, and he scratches my scalp. "It's not a dream, sweetheart. We came a week early because Wes kept begging. I think he missed you the most, if that's even possible."

Oh, Wes. He always was the most sensitive of the bunch. Such a sweetheart. The video game loving, snarky guy with the hardened exterior turned out to be the cinnamon roll of the group. Who would have thought?

"Sara and I played rock, paper, scissors for who got to come get you, though. I won, obviously. She's still pretty upset about it. But hey, I'm the captain. I could have just pulled rank, anyway."

"You wouldn't," I say with a snicker.

"Oh, I totally would."

I pull away from his embrace and choke back more tears. At least these are happy tears this time. He wipes my cheeks dry and beams at me like a puppy with a new squeak toy.

"But you're a whole week early. What are you going to do in the meantime?" I ask.

"I thought maybe you'd like to come aboard the ship, for starters. And then maybe if you're feeling up to it… we could go star gazing?"

I look down at myself and snort. "I'm still in my pajamas."

"You look cute the way you are, but if you want to change, I'll wait. But just know that you probably won't be wearing anything for very long," he says with a wink. He holds his hand out for me to take, and I smile at him.

"I can live with that," I say. "And after the con? What then?"

Aiden's expression softens as he tucks a strand of hair behind my ear. "The three of us thought we'd try living here for a little while. See how it goes."

I nearly choke on my own saliva. "What? You're going to live here? What about Twyla? And your people? You can't just leave them."

"Our people are in a good place now, thanks to you. They're grateful to you, and always will be. They've given us their blessing to stay here. You have friends, family. We don't want to pull you away from them."

I nibble my bottom lip, still unable to believe my eyes and ears. Is Aiden really here? And is he really suggesting he and the others live here, permanently?

"You have friends and family, too, though."

He chuckles as he slides his palms into his pockets. "Yeah, but… visiting them isn't difficult. Not for us. We want to do this, Taryn. We already agreed. You're stuck with us for as long as you'll tolerate our presence."

I roll my eyes and nudge him in the ribs playfully. "Well, I suppose we can try it. See how it goes. But this apartment isn't really big enough for the four of us. We'll probably have to find someplace else to live."

"There's always the ship," he suggests. "It has cloaking. No one will ever be the wiser."

"You want me to live in the ship? With that mattress?" I scoff, and for a second he peers at me with concern. He thinks I'm being serious, and then I break out into a large grin. "I guess if I have to."

"We won't even charge you rent. How about that?"

I shift my weight from side to side as I pretend to give his offer some serious consideration.

"Well, alright. That sounds okay."

He takes my hands into his and sways them gently back and forth. We stand like that for several minutes, just looking into each other's eyes, until Aiden's wrist thingy flickers to life with a loud chime.

"Aiden, is everything okay in there? Give us an update, please," Sara's voice comes through the device loud and clear. It's been an entire year without hearing her voice, and my heart leaps into my throat at the beautiful sound.

Aiden brings the device up to his mouth and says, "Everything is fine, Sara. I have Taryn and we'll be coming on board. Beam us up in thirty seconds, please."

There's a long pause on the other end, and for a second I think maybe she didn't get the message. And then she says, "Sorry. Wes was too busy losing his shit in the background, and I had to calm him down. You got it. I'm going to triangulate your position, so try not to move."

"Got it," he replies, then looks down at me. "It'll tingle and feel weird, but—"

"This better not be like the time I felt like I was getting ripped in half."

He winces. "Would it be a deal breaker if it was?"

"Not in the least," I say dryly, and give his hands a good, firm squeeze.

I take one last look around my apartment. These walls hold so many memories. Some good, some bad, but all mine. The future may always be one giant question mark to me, but for once in my life I'm happy and free to make as many mistakes as I can while I figure out what it is I want. And hey, at least my lease ends in a few weeks, anyway. The timing couldn't have been more perfect.

As the hair rises on my arms and the walls of the apartment begin to melt all around me, I can't keep from smiling. I waited an entire year for this, to be with the three people who I cherished more than anyone. I close my eyes and wait for the world around me to vanish. When I open them again, the first thing I see are Sara and Wes with their eyes so full of love that my heart breaks in the very best way possible.

"Hey," I whisper. "I'm home."

Acknowledgements

Thank you to my beta readers, Alistair Quinn and Christopher Clingerman. Without your help and encouragement, this book wouldn't have been possible. Thank you to my wonderful readers and newsletter subscribers. You mean the world to me, and you're the reason I keep writing. Thank you from the bottom of my heart.

I would also like to thank Teresa over at Wolf Sparrow Covers for the fun writing prompt! When she posted the cover to her social media, I knew I had to use it. I wasn't sure what the story was going to entail, but it didn't matter. I had to have that cover.

Did you enjoy this book?

Sign up to my newsletter to join my community.
Get a free short story just for signing up and be the first to know about new releases!

Spoiler Content Warnings

Hi there! If you're reading this, it's because you want to know exactly what you'll find in the pages of this book and don't mind being spoiled. I want to make sure you're going to have a good time with my book and make an informed choice before you encounter anything that might be a hard-pass for you. If you arrived here by accident and you DON'T want to see spoilers but still want a general content warning, there is one at the front of the book under the author's note!

End of a five-year-relationship at the start of the book. The heroine gets dumped via text message and later encounters her ex during the con. While the encounter comes and goes very quickly, it's not very pleasant.

Deception from the main alien trio. The trio hides their true identity from Taryn for a while. One of them tries to come clean before any sexual encounters begin, but Taryn doesn't believe them. The aliens are under the impression she does believe their admission before having sex. Some miscommunication happens.

Needles. While not explicit in content, needles do make a brief appearance during the Chimera Con blood drive.

Blood. Blood is depicted in the blood drive.

Aliens. Two gray aliens (like on the cover) and one alien with scales.

Graphic sexual content. This is basically a sex book. There's a *lot* of consensual sex, and a lot of naughty language is used. Face fucking, light BDSM elements, double penetration, orgasm denial, and lots and lots of coming are on the pages here. If you aren't into graphic depictions of sex, this may not be the book for you.

Space travel. A large portion of the book takes place inside an alien spacecraft. The men in black are also briefly mentioned.

Light BDSM/soft dom. Sara is a soft dom and makes use of nipple clamps and a probe. There is aftercare.

Polyamory. It's a big theme of the book. The three aliens and Taryn fall in love with each other.

Shitty corporate bosses. I tried to keep this book as light and fun as possible, but some real-world bullshit occurs in the form of a crappy job.